Heinrich Heine

**Lyrics and Ballads of Heine and other German Poets**

Heinrich Heine

**Lyrics and Ballads of Heine and other German Poets**

ISBN/EAN: 9783337128203

Printed in Europe, USA, Canada, Australia, Japan

Cover: Foto ©Andreas Hilbeck / pixelio.de

More available books at **www.hansebooks.com**

# LYRICS AND BALLADS

OF

# HEINE

## AND OTHER GERMAN POETS

TRANSLATED BY

## FRANCES HELLMAN

## G. P. PUTNAM'S SONS

NEW YORK
27 West Twenty-third Street

LONDON
24 Bedford Street, Strand

The Knickerbocker Press

1892

Printed and Bound by
The Knickerbocker Press, New York
G. P. Putnam's Sons

# TO MY MOTHER

# CONTENTS

## HEINE

v

## ROMANCES   *ROMANZEN*

## SONNET   *SONETTE*

## LYRICAL INTERLUDE
## *LYRISCHES INTERMEZZO*

## THE HOMEWARD JOURNEY
### *DIE HEIMKEHR*

THE HARTZ JOURNEY        *DIE HARZREISE*

## NORTHSEA CYCLE NORDSEE CYCLUS

### ANGÉLIQUE

### KATHARINE

## POEMS OF THE TIMES    *ZEITGEDICHTE*

## NEW SONGS    *NEUE LIEDER*

# GOETHE

## POEMS    *GEDICHTE*

# HEINE.

# Prologue.

*VORREDE.*

THIS is the fairy-wood of old !
  Sweet linden-buds are blowing !
The wondrous moonlight o'er my soul
  A magic spell is throwing.

I walked along, and as I walked
  Soft strains on high were ringing.
It is the nightingale !  Of love
  And love's great woe she 's singing.

She sings of love and love's great woe,
  Of laughter and of weeping ;
So sad is her rapture, so glad is her sob,
  Dreams wake, that long were sleeping.

I walked along, and as I walked
  In a clearing rose before me
A palace vast, whose gables seemed
  To soar toward heaven, o'er me.

3

Closed were the windows ; all appeared
    By silence and grief o'ertaken,
As tho' still death its home had made
    Within those walls forsaken.


Before the gate there lay a sphinx,
    Both horror and lust inviting ;
A woman's head and breast, to paws
    And trunk of lion uniting.


A glorious woman !   Her marble glance
    Spoke yearnings wild and tender,
Her arching lips said not a word,
    But smiled a mute surrender.


So sweetly sang the nightingale,
    I yielded to her wooing ;
And as I kissed that lovely face
    I sealed my own undoing.


The marble image warmed to life,
    The stone with moans resounded ;
She drank my kisses' ardent fire
    With thirst and greed unbounded.

She almost drained my breath—until
  Voluptuously bending,
She clasped me tight, her lion's claws
  My hapless body rending.


Delicious torture !   Rapturous woe !
  Infinite anguish and blessing !
Her claws inflict most fearful wounds,
  While her kiss on my mouth she is pressing !


The nightingale sang : "Oh, beautiful sphinx !
  Oh, love ! why is 't intended
That with the agony of death
  Thy bliss should all be blended ?


"Oh, lovely sphinx ! oh, solve for me
  The riddle strange past telling !
For many thousand years my thoughts
  Upon it have been dwelling."

# Dream Pictures.

## TRAUMBILDER.

---

## In Nightly Dream.

### IM NÄCHT'GEN TRAUM'.

IN nightly dream I once myself did see,
  Black coat, silk vest, and every preparation,
Down to the cuffs—as for some celebration.
My lovely darling then confronted me.
I bowed and said : " May you the fair bride be ?
Why then, my dear, take my congratulation ! "
But oh ! those words nigh caused my strangulation.
They fell so stiff, so cold, so haughtily
Upon mine ear.   And bitter tears came streaming
Out from my darling's eyes.   And that flood's power
Swept far from me the vision brightly gleaming.
Oh ! tender eyes, love's stars that glow so kindly,
What tho' in dreams and many a waking hour
You oft deceived me ?   Yet I trust you blindly !

# ¶ Lay and Slept Most Peacefully.

*ICH LAG UND SCHLIEF UND SCHLIEF RECHT MILD.*

I LAY and slept most peacefully,
   Gone was all strife and care ;
A vision then appeared to me,
   The maid of all most fair.

Like unto marble she was white,
   And  weirdly lovely she ;
Her eyes gleamed with a pearly light,
   Her hair waved wondrously.

And softly, softly then comes on
   That maiden marble white,
And then close to my heart lies down
   That maiden marble white.

How starts and throbs my burning heart
   With pain and ecstasy !
The fair one's does not throb nor start,—
   Ice could not colder be.

" My heart nor throbs, nor starts, 't is true,
   Ice could not colder be,
But I have felt love's rapture too
   And love's great mastery.

" On cheeks and lips there gleams no red,
   No warm blood flows thro' me,—
But do not shrink away in dread,
   For I am fond of thee."

More fierce grew her caress,—until
   She clasped me all too tight.
The cock crowed loud,—then vanished, still,
   That maiden marble white.

## Many Pale Spectres Long Vanished.

*ICH HAB' VIEL' BLASSE LEICHEN.*

MANY pale spectres, long vanished,
    I evoked by a word's magic might ;
And now they will not be banished
    Again to their former night.

The master's words, all-compelling,
    I forgot in my dread and dismay ;
And now to their shadowy dwelling
    My own ghosts would lead me away.

Dark demons, cease your persistence !
    Begone, and press not so close !
For many a joy of existence
    May yet bloom in the light of the rose.

Oh ! could I once only press her
    Quite close to my glowing breast,
On cheeks and on lips caress her,
    With kisses of anguish most blest !

Oh ! could I but once hear her saying
    A single word, loving and low,—
Then, spirits, without more delaying
    With you to your dark home I 'd go !

The spirits one and all hear me,
    And nod appallingly.
My darling, now I am near thee ;—
    My darling, lov'st thou me ?

# Songs.

## *LIEDER.*

———

## At Morn I Rise and Query.

*MORGENS STEH' ICH AUF UND FRAGE.*

A<sup>T</sup> morn I rise and query :
   " Will sweetheart come to-day ? "
At night I sink down weary :
   " Again she 's stayed away."

All night, alone with my sorrow
   A sleepless watch I keep ;
I wander about on the morrow
   As though I were half asleep.

13

# To the Woods My Footsteps Turning.

*ICH WANDELTE UNTER DEN BÄUMEN.*

TO the woods my footsteps turning,
   I strolled with my grief, apart ;
And then the old dream's yearning
   Crept back into my heart.

That little word,—who did bring it ?
   Say, birdies, that heavenward soar !
—Oh, hush ! for my heart, when you sing it,
   Aches twice as much as before.

" A maiden who passed here, has taught it :
   She sang it, and we heard ;
And so, we birdies have caught it,
   That lovely, golden word."

Nevermore such a tale be revealing,
   Oh ! cunning songsters, ye !
My sorrow you fain would be stealing,
   But none can my confidant be.

# Fairest Cradle of My Sorrow.

*SCHÖNE WIEGE MEINER LEIDEN.*

FAIREST cradle of my sorrow,
  Fairest grave of peace to me,
Fairest town, ere dawns the morrow
  We must part,—farewell to thee.

Fare thee well, O threshold lowly,
  Where my darling's footsteps rest,
Fare thee well, O spot most holy,
  Where she first my vision blest.

Had I but beheld thee never,
  Thou, my heart's belovèd queen,
Then it had not happened ever
  That so wretched I had been.

For thy heart I have not striven,
  Nor to gain thy love have tried ;
All my longing was to live in
  Quiet, where thou dost abide.

But I leave at thy own urging ;
From thy lips harsh sayings pour ;
Madness in my breast is surging,
And my heart is sick and sore.

With my staff I drag on, dreary,
Limbs that weaken day by day
Till I lay my head, a-weary,
In a cool grave, far away.

# First I Felt Nigh to Despairing.

*ANFANGS WOLLT' ICH FAST VERZAGEN.*

FIRST, I felt nigh to despairing,—
    Thought I could not bear my lot;
Yet my lot I have been bearing,
    Only how,—pray ask me not!

# Romances.

## ROMANZEN.

———

## The Mourner.

### DER TRAURIGE.

EVERY heart with woe is smitten
   When the sad youth they behold
On whose face are plainly written
   Pain and sorrows manifold.

Breezes soft, with pity laden,
   Gently fan his fevered brow ;
Many erst so coy a maiden
   Longs, with smiles, to soothe him now.

From the city's noisy bustle
   To the woods he hies away ;
There the tree-tops gaily rustle,
   And the birds sing carols gay.

19

But the song soon dies out wholly,
　　Tree and leaf both sadly sway,
As the mournful youth, now slowly,
　　Near the forest wends his way.

# The Mountain=Voice.

*DIE BERGSTIMME.*

ACROSS the vale, in slow, sad pace,
  There rides a trooper brave ;
" Oh ! go I now to sweetheart's arms,
  Or to a gloomy grave ?"
  The mountain answer gave :
    " A gloomy grave."

And onward still the horseman rides,
  And sighs with heaving breast ;
" So soon I go then to my grave,
  Ah well, the grave brings rest."
  The mountain-voice confessed :
    " The grave brings rest."

And then, down from the horseman's cheek
  A woeful tear-drop fell ;
" And if the grave alone brings rest,
  All will, in the grave, be well."
  The voice—with hollow knell :
    " In the grave be well."

# Poor Peter.

*DER ARME PETER.*

AS Hans and Grete join in dance
   And shout in wildest glee,
So sad and silent Peter stands—
   As white as chalk is he.


Now, bride and groom are Gret' and Hans
   All decked in wedding-gilt ;
A' biting his nails poor Peter stands,
   And wears his workman's kilt.


To himself, in secret, Peter said,
   And sadly gazed on the two :
" Oh ! had I not so wise a head,
   Some harm to myself I 'd do !


" For in my heart there 's such great woe,
   It fain would burst my breast ;
Where'er I stand, where'er I go,
   It never lets me rest.

' It drives me to my Grete sweet
  As if she 'd cure my pain ;
But when my eyes her glances meet,
  It drives me forth again.

" I climb up to the mountain-top ;
  —Alone one there can be,—
And there, quite silently, I stop,
  And weep, quite silently."

.    .    .    .    .    .

Poor Peter staggers slowly' by
  So deathly pale, and wan, and shy ;
And all the people whom he meets,
  Stand still, to watch him, in the streets.

The maidens whisper secretly :
  " Out of the grave, no doubt, comes he."
Oh, no, you little damsels fair,
  He 's just about to enter there !

As he has lost his own sweetheart,
  The grave 's the place to lie apart ;
Where he may pass the years away
  And sleep until the judgment-day.

# The Message.

*DIE BOTSCHAFT.*

UP, up, my boy, and saddle quick,
　　And fling thee on thy steed,
And to King Duncan's castle ride
　　Thro' woods and fields, with speed.

Slip in his stable there, and wait
　　Till by the groom espied ;
Then question him : " Say which one is
　　Of Duncan's daughters bride ? "

If says the boy : " The brown one 't is."
　　Then quickly let me know ;
But if he says : " The blonde one 't is,"
　　Thou need'st not hurry so.

To Master Twinester then go out,
　　Buy me a rope there, and—
Ride slowly back, say not a word,
　　But lay that in my hand.

# Sonnet.

## SONETTE.

---

## To My Mother.

### AN MEINE MUTTER.

I HAVE been wont my head to carry high,
  My will has been my law in every thing ;
  If opposite to me there stood a king
I would not timidly avert mine eye.
But, Mother dear, I 'll tell thee openly :
  However haughtily my soul may swell,
  When in thy presence sweet and dear I dwell,
A trembling diffidence comes over me.
  Am I subdued by thy great spirit's might,
  Thy pure, keen soul that fathoms all aright,
  And, flashing forth, soars up to heaven's light ?
Do recollections rise to torture me,
The many deeds with which I grievously

Thy dear heart pained, that loved me tenderly ?

    .     .     .     .         .

In frenzy wild I once deserted thee ;
   The wish to know the whole world filled my
      mind ;
   I longed to see if love I there could find,—
That love I might encompass lovingly !
I sought love in all streets ; at every gate,
   In suppliance outstretched, I held my palms,
   And begged for just a little of love's alms,—
But all they gave me, laughing, was cold hate !
   Yet still I sought for love ; again
   My endless search resumed.   But all in vain.
Then homeward turned I, sick, with troubled
      thought.
   But there, to bid me welcome, thou wert nigh,
   And lo ! what I saw shining in thine eye,
That was the sweet love I so long had sought !

# Lyrical Interlude.

---

## 'T Was in the Glorious Month of May.

*IM WUNDERSCHÖNEN MONAT MAI.*

'T WAS in the glorious month of May
 When all the buds were blowing,
I first felt in my bosom
 Love's tender fire glowing.

'T was in the glorious month of May
 When all the birds were singing,
The yearning deep I told her
 That in my heart was ringing !

## Up From My Tears, Fair Flowers.

*AUS MEINEN THRÄNEN SPRIESSEN.*

UP from my tears, fair flowers,
    Innumerable, rise ;
The nightingales' sweet chorus
    Re-echoes in my sighs.

And if thou lov'st me, darling,
    All the flowers to thee I 'll bring
And then beneath thy window
    The nightingales shall sing.

# The Rose and the Lily, the Sun and the Dove.

*DIE ROSE, DIE LILIE, DIE TAUBE, DIE SONNE.*

THE rose and the lily, the sun and the dove,
   I loved them all once with a rapturous love.
I love them no more, I love her alone,
The rarest, the fairest, the dearest, the one ;
She herself is the fountain whence all rapture flows,
She 's the lily, the dove, the sun, and the rose.

## When I Can Gaze into Thine Eyes.

*WENN ICH IN DEINE AUGEN SEH'.*

WHEN I can gaze into thine eyes,
　　All pain, all sorrow from me flies ;
But when my lips thy kisses meet,
　　Then is, indeed, my cure complete !

When I can lean against thy breast,
　　With heav'nly calm my soul is blest ;
But when thou sayest : " I love thee,"
　　Then must I weep most bitterly.

# Thy Visage Beautiful and Kind.

*DEIN ANGESICHT SO LIEB UND SCHÖN.*

THY visage, beautiful and kind,
   Appeared, in dreams, before my mind ;
With angel's softest light it shone,
   And yet so pale, so woe-begone.

Thy lips alone were rosy bright ;
   But soon cold Death will kiss them white,
And from thine eyes, the heav'nly ray
   That gently beams, will fade away.

## Oh! Lean Thy Cheek Against My Cheek.

*LEHN' DEINE WANG' AN MEINE WANG'.*

OH ! lean thy cheek against my cheek,
  Together our tears will flow then ;
Thy heart press close against my heart,
  Together our flames will glow then.

And when the great stream of our tears
  Flows into the mighty fire,
And when I clasp thee in strong embrace,
  With yearning love I 'll expire !

## The Stars have Stood for Ages.

*ES STEHEN UNBEWEGLICH.*

THE stars have stood for ages
   Immovably above ;
And gazed upon each other
   With yearning, woeful love.

They speak a certain language,
   So beautiful, so fine,
That none of all the masters
   Its meaning can divine.

But I have learnt that language,
   Which naught from my mind can erase ;
The grammar in which I studied,
   Was my lovely sweetheart's face.

## On the Wings of Song I 'll Carry.

*AUF FLÜGELN DES GESANGES.*

ON the wings of song I 'll carry
  Thee, darling, off with me ;
On the Ganges' shores we 'll tarry,
  No spot can lovelier be.

A garden with rose-red bowers,
  In the moonlight calm lies there ;
And there the lotus-flowers
  Await their sister fair.

The violets titter, caressing,
  And gaze at the stars, on high ;
And fairy-tales are confessing
  The roses, whispering shy.

To hearken, then come leaping
  The gentle, wise gazelles ;
The sacred river's sweeping
  Far out, in the distance, swells.

And there we 'll sink down lowly
   Beneath the great palm-tree ;
Drink love and peace most holy
   In dreams of ecstasy.

## To Steep My Very Spirit.

*ICH WILL MEINE SEELE TAUCHEN.*

TO steep my very spirit
    In a lily's heart, I long ;
That softly I may hear it
    Exhale my darling's song.

The song must tremble and quiver,
    Alike unto that kiss,
Of which she was the giver
    In an hour of wondrous bliss.

# The Lotus Flow'r Stands Trembling.

## DIE LOTUSBLUME ÄNGSTIGT.

THE lotus flow'r stands trembling
　　Beneath the sun's fierce light,
With head low bent, and dreaming,
　　She waits the coming night.

The moon, who is her lover,
　　Awakes her with his rays ;
To him she gladly unveileth
　　Her gentle, flower-face.

She blooms, and glows and glistens,
　　And mutely stares above ;
She weeps, exhales and trembles,
　　With the bliss and woes of love.

## Oh! do Not Swear, but Kiss Me, Dear.

*O SCHWÖRE NICHT UND KÜSSE NUR.*

OH! do not swear, but kiss me, dear,
All women's oaths are false, I fear ;
Thy words are sweet, but far more sweet
The kiss in which our lips did meet ;
That kiss is mine, in it trust I,
But words, like mist, float idly by.

Oh ! swear on, dear, eternally !
Thy simple word suffices me.
I sink upon thy bosom fair
And deem that I am blessèd there,
And that, through all eternity,
And longer still, thou 'lt love but me !

## ¶ Nurse No Wrath, and Though My Heart be Crushed.

*ICH GROLLE NICHT, UND WENN DAS HERZ AUCH
BRICHT.*

### I.

I NURSE no wrath, and though my heart be
crushed,
Oh ! love forever lost, my wrath is hushed !
Though thy fair form be decked with jewels bright,
No single ray illumes thy spirit's night.

I 've known this long.   For in my sleep
I saw thee, and thy bosom's gloomy deep,
And saw the viper gnawing at thy heart,
And saw how wretched, oh ! my love, thou art.

### II.

Yes, thou art wretched, and I 'll not complain.
My love, we both must ever wretched be ;
Till death has rent our two poor hearts in twain,
My love, we both must ever wretched be.

I see the scoff that on thy proud lip dwells,
    I see thy glance flare out disdainfully,
I see how haughtily thy bosom swells—
    Yet thou art wretched, wretched just like me.

Thy quivering mouth a secret pain reveals,
    Through unshed tears thine eye can scarcely see ;
Thy haughty breast a hidden wound conceals,—
    My love, we both must ever wretched be.

# And Could the Little Flowers Know.

*UND WÜSSTEN'S DIE BLUMEN, DIE KLEINEN.*

AND could the little flowers know
  How pierced my heart with grief,
I 'm sure their tears with mine would flow  ⁃
  To bring my pain relief.

And if the nightingales but knew
  How sick I am, and sad,
They, lustily, would sound anew
  Their carols bright and glad.

And if the golden stars, on high,
  My sorrow could but guess,
They would come down out of the sky
  To comfort my distress.

Not one of these can know my pain,
  One only knows its smart ;
For she herself has rent in twain,
  Has rent in twain my heart !

# Why Do the Roses Look So Pale?

*WARUM SIND DENN DIE ROSEN SO BLASS?*

WHY do the roses look so pale,
   Oh ! darling, tell me why ?
The violets blue, in yon green vale,
   Why are they mute and shy ?

Why chants the lark in plaintive wise,
   As it soars aloft on its way ?
From balsam-herbs why does there rise
   A scent of death's decay ?

Why does the sun on meads display
   Such cold and frowning gloom ?
And wherefore is the earth so gray
   And dreary as the tomb ?

Why am e'en I, so sick, so weak,
   My lovely love, oh ! say ?
Oh ! speak, my best belovèd, speak,
   Why hast thou gone away ?

## So Many Tales They Bore Thee.

*SIE HABEN DIR VIEL ERZÄHLET.*

SO many tales they bore thee,
   And oft of me complained,
But never set before thee
   What most my heart has pained.

They made much ado, and sadly
   They shook their heads as grieved ;
They spoke of me so badly,—
   And thou hast all believed.

But what was the very saddest,
   Not one of them has guessed ;
The saddest and the maddest
   Lies hidden in my breast.

## The Linden Blossomed, the Nightingale Sung.

*DIE LINDE BLÜHTE, DIE NACHTIGALL SANG.*

THE linden blossomed, the nightingale sung,
   The sun laughed forth with joyful face ;
You kissed me then, and your arms 'round me flung
   As you pressed me close in fond embrace.

The leaves all fell with the raven's cry,
   The sun frowned down in dismallest plight ;
We then bade each other an icy good-by,
   And politely you curtsied a bow most polite.

## Because So Long, So Long I Stayed.

*UND ALS ICH SO LANGE, SO LANGE GESÄUMT.*

BECAUSE so long, so long I stayed
In foreign lands, and dreamed and played,
My sweetheart's patience all gave way ;
She sewed a gown for her wedding-day,
And clasped to her arms in wedlock's joys
The most stupid of all the stupid boys.

So fair my love is, and so kind,
Her vision sweet lives in my mind ;
The violet eyes, the red cheeks dear,
They glow and bloom year after year ;
That I left such a darling verily is
The most stupid of all my stupidities.

# A Pine=Tree Standeth Lonely.

*EIN FICHTENBAUM STEHT EINSAM.*

A PINE-TREE standeth lonely
    In the north, on a barren height ;
It slumbers, in snow and ice clad,
    As in a mantle white.

It dreameth of a palm-tree
    That, silent and alone,
In distant Orient mourneth,
    On a burning ridge of stone.

## The Head Speaks.

*DER KOPF SPRICHT.*

COULD I the little footstool be
Which holds my love's feet twain,
If e'er so hard she stamped on me,
Indeed, I 'd not complain.

## The Heart Speaks.

*DAS HERZ SPRICHT.*

OH ! could I but the cushion be
Through which her needles go,
If e'er so hard she then pierced me,
The pain would please me so.

## The Song Speaks.

*DAS LIED SPRICHT.*

OH ! were the scrap of paper I
With which her curls she wreathes,
I 'd whisper to her, on the sly,
What in me lives and breathes.

# Up from the Tomb Rise Pictures.

*MANCH BILD VERGESS'NER ZEITEN.*

UP from the tomb rise pictures
   Of the long-forgotten past,
To me my life recalling
   When near thine it was cast.

All day I wandered, dreaming,
   Ever from street to street ;
The people stood and marvelled
   One so mute and sad to meet.

At night things seemed much better,
   For then the streets were bare ;
And I and my shadow, we wander'd
   Together in silence there.

With footsteps that re-echoed
   I crossed the bridge straightway,
And the moon came out to send me
   A grave, but friendly, ray.

At thy house, at length, I halted,
    And lifted my gaze on high ;
And fastened it on thy window,—
    To breaking my heart was nigh !

I know that from thy casement
    Thou 'st look'd down many a night,
Seeing me stand like a pillar
    In the rays of the pale moonlight.

## A Youth Once Loved a Maiden.

*EIN YÜNGLING LIEBT EIN MÄDCHEN.*

A YOUTH once loved a maiden
    Who did another prefer ;
That other loved still another
    And plighted his troth to her.

The maiden married in anger,
    The very first man who bore
Straight down upon her pathway ;
    The youth was smitten sore.

It is an old, old story,
    And yet, 't is ever new ;
And the heart that, by chance, it striketh,
    Is broken right in two,

## Whene'er I hear the Little Song.

*HÖR' ICH DAS LIEDCHEN KLINGEN.*

WHENE'ER I hear the little song
    That once my sweetheart sang,
It seems as if my heart must break,
    So bitter is its pang.

A nameless longing drives me forth,—
    To the woodland heights I go ;
And there, in bitter tears, dissolves
    My overwhelming woe.

## A Princess Came in Dreams to Me.

*MIR TRÄUMTE VON EINEM KÖNIGS-KIND.*

A PRINCESS came in dreams to me
    With wet and pallid face ;
We sat beneath the linden-tree
    Close-clasped in love's embrace.

" I do not want thy father's throne,
    Nor his golden sceptre rare,
His diamond crown I would not own,
    But thy sweet self, so fair."

" That may not be," said she to me,
    " For I lie in my grave below,
At night alone I come to thee
    Because I love thee so."

# Thou 'st Ever had and hast My Heart.

*ICH HAB' DICH GELIEBET UND LIEBE DICH NOCH.*

THOU 'ST ever had and hast my heart ;
   Were the world one funeral pyre,
Out of its very wreck would dart
   My love's consuming fire.

And after I have loved but thee
   Until my hour of doom,
I 'll take my great love-wound with me,
   To the eternal tomb.

## On a Radiant Summer=Morning.

*AM LEUCHTENDEN SOMMERMORGEN.*

ON a radiant summer-morning
   About the garden I stray ;
The flowers talk and whisper—
   I have not a word to say.

The flowers talk and whisper,
   With pity my face they scan ;
" Oh ! be not wroth with our sister,
   Thou sad and pallid man ! "

## My Love Shines Out in Its Glory.

*ES LEUCHTET MEINE LIEBE.*

MY love shines out in its glory
    O'ercast by a darkened light,
Like a mournful fairy story
    That is told on a summer's night.

" In a magic garden two lovers
    Walk alone, and say not a word ;
The moonlight over them hovers
    And the nightingales are heard.

" The maid stands with unmoved glances,
    At her feet the Knight she sees ;
Then the Desert Giant advances,
    And the frightened maiden flees.

" On the ground the Knight falls, dying ;
    The giant stalks back to his home "—
When I in my grave am lying
    The end of that tale will have come.

# They Caused Me Greatest Torture.

*SIE HABEN MICH GEQUÄLET.*

THEY caused me greatest torture
   Till I nearly cursed my fate,
Some of them with their loving,
   And others with their hate.

My very drink they poisoned,
   They poisoned the bread I ate,
Some of them with their loving,
   And others with their hate.

But she who, beyond all others,
   Pained, grieved and tortured me,—
By her I ne'er was hated
   Nor ever loved she me.

# There Lies the Warmth of Summer.

*ES LIEGT DER HEISSE SOMMER.*

THERE lies the warmth of summer
  Upon thy little face ;
In thy little heart cold winter
  Has found its resting-place.

Some day all this will alter
  Oh, dear belovèd mine !
On thy cheeks will lie the winter,
  In thy heart will summer shine.

# ¶ Don't Believe in the heaven.

*ICH GLAUB' NICHT AN DEN HIMMEL.*

I DON'T believe in the heaven
  Of which the dominies speak,
I believe but in thy glances,
  They hold the heaven I seek.

I don't believe in the Godhead
  Which priestly words imply,
I believe but in thy heart, love,
  No other God have I.

I don't believe in the devil,
  In hell, or its fiery smart ;
I believe but in thy glances,
  And in thy wicked heart.

# When Two Take Leave of Each Other.

*WENN ZWEI VON EINANDER SCHEIDEN.*

WHEN two take leave of each other,
    Each presses the other's hand,
And then they fall to weeping,
    And sighing without end.

We did not shed a tear-drop,
    We did not sigh or moan,—
The weeping and the sighing
    Came when we were alone.

# ¶ Wept Whilst ¶ Was Dreaming.

*ICH HAB' IM TRAUM' GEWEINET.*

I WEPT whilst I was dreaming—
　I dreamt they 'd laid thee low ;
I woke,—and still the tear-drop
　Adown my cheek did flow.

I wept whilst I was dreaming,—
　I dreamt thou 'dst gone from me ;
I woke,—and still I wept on
　A long time, bitterly.

I wept whilst I was dreaming,—
　I dreamt thou still lov'dst me ;
I woke,—and yet my tear-flow
　Streams on unceasingly.

# At Night in Dreams I See Thee, When.

*ALLNÄCHTLICH IM TRAUME SEH' ICH DICH.*

AT night in dreams I see thee, when
So kindly thou dost greet ;
And weeping loud I fling me then
Down at thy dear, dear feet.

Thy gaze is such a pitying one,
Thy small blonde head shakes no,
And slowly from thine eyes there run
The pearly drops of woe.

Thou giv'st me a bunch of cypress flow'rs,
And a whispered word is heard ;—
I wake ! Gone is the bunch of flow'rs
And forgotten is the word !

## The Autumn=Wind Rattles the Branches.

*DER HERBSTWIND RÜTTELT DIE BÄUME.*

THE autumn-wind rattles the branches,
   The night is cold and chill ;
I ride, in my gray cloak folded,
   Through the woods alone and still.

And as I ride, my fancies
   Are riding on before ;
They waft me lightly onward,
   Up to my sweetheart's door.

The dogs are barking, the servants
   Their lighted candles bring ;
I rush up the winding staircase,
   My steel spurs rattle and ring.

In the brightly-curtained chamber
   All is so fragrant and warm ;
And there my love awaits me,—
   I fly into her arm.

The wind wails low, and the oak-tree
To speak these words doth seem :
" What wilt thou, foolish horseman,
With such a foolish dream ? "

# A Star Comes Downward Falling.

*ES FÄLLT EIN STERN HERUNTER.*

A STAR comes downward falling
    Out of its glittering height,
It is the star of true love
    On which my eyes alight.

Blossoms and leaves in plenty
    Fall from the apple-tree ;
Then come the mischievous breezes
    And toss them playfully.

On the pond the swan is singing,
    And paddling to and fro ;
With dying voice he diveth
    To the watery grave below.

All 's dark and still, and the blossoms
    And leaves are scattered like spray ;
The star flew crackling to pieces,
    And the song has died away.

## Night Brooded on Mine Eyelids.

*NACHT LAG AUF MEINEN AUGEN.*

NIGHT brooded on mine eyelids,
　　Upon my mouth lay lead ;
With head and heart grown rigid,
　　In my grave I lay as dead.

I do not well remember,
　　How long I slept in gloom,
I wakened up—and heard then
　　A knocking at my tomb.

" Wilt not arise, O Henry,
　　The judgment-day comes on,
The dead are all arisen,
　　Eternal joys begun."

I can't arise, my darling,
　　For I am blinded still
By all the bitter tear-drops
　　That once mine eyes did fill.

" But I will kiss thee, Henry,
  And drive night from thine eyes,
That thou may'st see the angels
  And the light of Paradise."

I can't arise, my darling,
  For still the blood flows free
From my poor heart, once wounded
  By one sharp word from thee.

" My hand I 'll lay quite gently,
  Oh ! Henry, on thy heart ;
Then will it cease its bleeding,
  And cured will be its smart."

I can't arise, my darling,
  My head is bleeding too ;
For when they stole thee from me,
  I shot it through and through.

" With mine own tresses, Henry,
  I 'll stop the fountain red,
With them, I 'll check the blood-stream,
  And heal thy wounded head."

The voice so soft, so sweet was,
    I could not answer no ;
I tried forthwith to raise me,—
    To my love I fain would go.

But oh ! all of a sudden,
    With a gush, the old wounds broke.
From head and heart the blood streamed—
    And lo ! there I awoke !

## The Old Unhappy Ditties.

*DIE ALTEN, BÖSEN LIEDER.*

THE old unhappy ditties,
   The dreams with bitter sting,
All these now let us bury ;
   A mighty coffin bring.

But what I shall lay in it,
   As yet, I 'll tell no one ;
The coffin must be larger
   Than Heidelberg's great tun.

And bring a death-bier with it,
   Of planks both thick and strong ;
This bier must be still longer
   Than Mayence' bridge is long.

And bring me then twelve giants
   Who greater strength have shown
Than Christopher, the saintly,
   In the Minster of Cologne.

This coffin they must carry
  And sink beneath the wave ;
For such a mighty coffin
  Must have a mighty grave.

But know ye why this coffin
  So heavy and strong may be ?
In it my love lies buried
  And all my misery.

# The Homeward Journey.

*DIE HEIMKEHR.*

---

## I Know Not What Has Come O'er Me.

*ICH WEISS NICHT WAS SOLL ES BEDEUTEN.*

I KNOW not what has come o'er me
   That I am so sad to-day,
An old tale rises before me,
   I cannot drive it away.

It is cool, and the day declineth,
   And tranquil the Rhine flows on ;
The crest of the mountain shineth
   In the glow of the evening sun.

Up there, in glamour entrancing
   Sits a maiden, wondrous fair ;
Her golden jewels are glancing,
   She combeth her golden hair.

71

With golden comb her tresses
  She combs, and a lay sings she
That bewilders and caresses
  With mighty melody.

Wild woe in his bosom burning
  The youth, in his boat, drifts by ;
He sees not the whirlpool turning,
  His gaze is fastened on high.

Methinks the waves will have swallowed
  Both boat and boatman anon ;—
And this, with her song unhallowed,
  The Loreley hath done.

# My Heart, My Heart Is Mournful.

*MEIN HERZ, MEIN HERZ IST TRAURIG.*

MY heart, my heart is mournful,
  Yet laughs the bright May-sky ;
I lean against the linden
  On the bastion old and high.

And calmly there, beneath me,
  Glides by the blue town-moat ;
A boy is rowing and angling
  And whistling in his boat.

In bright and tiny medley
  Appear on yonder side
The villas, and gardens, and people,
  Woods, oxen, and meadows wide.

On the grass, to bleach their linen,
  The playful maidens come ;
The mill-wheel scatters diamonds,
  I hear its distant hum.

Against the gray old tower
  A sentry-box stands low,
A scarlet-coated fellow
  Is pacing to and fro.

He 's playing with his musket
  That in the sun gleams red ;
Now he presents and shoulders—
  I wish he 'd shoot me dead.

# Thou Lovely Fishermaiden.

*DU SCHÖNES FISCHERMÄDCHEN.*

THOU lovely fishermaiden,
  Come, drive thy skiff to land,
Come, sit thee down beside me,
  We 'll whisper hand in hand.

On my heart thy dear head pillow,
  Be not afraid of me ;
Dost thou not fearless venture
  Each day on the stormy sea ?

My heart is like the ocean,
  Has storm, and ebb and flow,
And many a pearl most precious
  Lies in its depths below.

## The Evening Shades Draw Slowly High.

*DER ABEND KOMMT GEZOGEN.*

THE evening shades draw slowly nigh,
  Dense mists the ocean screen,
Mysteriously the billows sigh,
  A white form then is seen.

The sea-maid comes on wat'ry crest,
  On the shore, by me, sits down ;
The surging of her snow-white breast
  Bursts through her gossamer gown.

She clasps me tight and close doth press,
  To take my breath away ;—
Oh, far too strong is thy caress,
  Thou lovely water-fay.

" My arms do press and clasp thee so,
  And tightly thee enfold,
Because near thee I 'd warmer grow,
  The night is far too cold."

Now pale and paler looks the moon
  Through veil'd clouds far away ;
More dim and wet thine eye has grown
  Thou lovely water-fay.

" My eye nor wet nor dimmer grows,
  It is so dim and wet,
Because when from the sea I rose
  A drop was left there yet."

The gulls in shrill complaining start,
  The wild sea breaks in spray ;—
So wild and quickly beats thy heart
  Thou lovely water-fay.

" In motion wild my heart I see,
  It beats so quick and wild,
For I love thee inexpressibly
  Thou lovely human child ! "

## Far Out in Radiance O'er the Sea.

*DAS MEER ERGLÄNZTE WEIT HINAUS.*

FAR out in radiance o'er the sea
  The parting sunlight shone,
Near the lonely fisher-hut sat we,
  We sat there mute and alone.

The mist came up, the tide rose high,
  The gull flew to and fro,
And lovingly, from out thine eye,
  Came tear-drops, falling low.

I saw them fall upon thy hand,
  Upon my knee I sank ;
And then from off thy dear white hand
  The tears away I drank.

My body since that hour doth fade,
  My soul dies longingly,—
For with her tears that hapless maid
  Alas ! has poisoned me !

## Upon the Far Horizon.

*AM FERNEN HORIZONTE.*

UPON the far horizon
  Looms, as in misty clouds,
The city, with its tower,
  In evening's twilight-shrouds.

A humid breeze casts ripples
  O'er waters gray and dark,
With stroke both sad and measured
  The boatman rows my bark.

Once more the sun glows radiant
  Before it sinks to rest,
To me the spot unveiling
  Where I lost what I love best.

## ¶ Stood in Gloomy Dreaming.

*ICH STAND IN DUNKELN TRÄUMEN.*

I STOOD in gloomy dreaming,
  Intent on her pictured form,
And the belovèd features
  With secret life grew warm.

About her lips there quivered
  A smile, in wondrous wise ;
What seemed like tears of sadness
  Was shining in her eyes.

And then my own tears, also,
  Came coursing silently,—
Alas ! I cannot believe it,
  That thou art lost to me !

# They Think That I Am Pining.

*MAN GLAUBT DASS ICH MICH GRÄME.*

THEY think that I am pining
  Of true love's bitter grief,
And I myself take part now
  In other folks' belief.

Thou large-eyed little darling,
  I 've said to thee alway,
That I love thee past all telling ;
  Love eats my heart away.

But only my still chamber
  Such words as these could hear,
Alas ! I was ever silent
  When thou, my love, wert near.

For there were evil spirits
  That kept my mouth shut tight ;
And ah ! those evil spirits
  Have now undone me quite.

## They Loved Each Other, but Neither.

*SIE LIEBTEN SICH BEIDE, DOCH KEINER.*

THEY loved each other, but neither
   Would to the other confess ;
Their looks were dark, but their bosoms
   Were melting with tenderness.

At last they parted, and only
   In dreams had meetings rare ;
They both long since had perished, —
   Though hardly themselves aware.

## My Heart Is Sad, and I Am Driven.

*DAS HERZ IST MIR BEDRÜCKT UND SEHNLICH.*

MY heart is sad, and I am driven
    To think of old times longingly,
The world was then so good to live in,
    And folks jogged on so peacefully.

But now confusion e'er grows strongér,
    There 's naught but struggle, strife, and dread ;
The God above us lives no longer,
    And down below the devil 's dead.

Of light and joy this has bereft us,
    All things look jangled, rotten, gray,
And were n't a little love still left us,
    Our last support were snatched away !

## Do Not Lose All Patience With Me.

*WERDET NUR NICHT UNGEDULDIG.*

DO not lose all patience with me
   If my olden heart-ache's sobbing
In the songs I now am singing
   Can be heard still plainly throbbing.

Wait, and you will hear this echo
   Of past grief resound no longer ;
And my songs' new spring will blossom
   In a heart grown calm and stronger.

# heart, Despair Not, I Implore It.

*HERZ, MEIN HERZ, SEI NICHT BEKLOMMEN.*

HEART, despair not, I implore it,
    Learn to bear thy fate's decree ;
That which winter took from thee
Spring, returning, will restore it.

Much is left that did not perish,
    Is not still the world most fair ?
    All thou findest lovely there,
All is thine, to love and cherish.

## Like to a Flower, Lovely.

*DU BIST WIE EINE BLUME.*

LIKE to a flower, lovely
    And pure and fair thou art ;
I gaze on thee, and sadness
    Then steals into my heart.

I long to lay in blessing
    My hands on thy head, and pray
That God keep thee so lovely
    So fair and pure alway.

## Child, It Would Be Thine Undoing.

*KIND, ES WÄRE DEIN VERDERBEN.*

CHILD, it would be thine undoing,
  And I try most earnestly
That thy heart so dear and tender
  Never glow with love of me.

But that I succeed so quickly,
  Almost makes my spirits fall ;
After all—at times I tell me,
  Could'st thou love me after all !

## Oh! That the Stream of My Sorrows.

*ICH WOLLT' MEINE SCHMERZEN ERGÖSSEN.*

OH! that the stream of my sorrows
  In a single word might flow;
To the merry breezes I 'd give it,
  That it merrily forth should go.

They 'd bear it to thee, belovèd,
  That sorrow-laden word,
At every place and hour,
  By thee it would be heard.

And when upon thine eyelids
  Sleep scarce has laid its hand,
My word will still pursue thee
  Into the dreamy land.

# In the Post=Chaise Dark We Journeyed.

*WIR FUHREN ALLEIN IM DUNKELN POST-*
*WAGEN DIE GANZE NACHT.*

IN the post-chaise dark we journeyed
   Alone, the whole night through ;
On each other's heart we rested,
   There jesting, and laughing too.

But when at length the day dawned,
   Dear child ! how surprised we were !
For Cupid was seated between us,
   The young blind passenger !

# The Pilgrimage to Kevlaar.

*DIE WALLFAHRT NACH KEVLAAR.*

### I.

THE mother stood at the window,
　　The son lay in his bed ;
" Here 's a procession, William ;
　　Wilt not look out ? " she said.

" I am so sick, O mother,
　　Can see and hear no more ;
I 'm thinking of dead Gretchen,
　　That makes my heart so sore."

" Arise, we 'll go to Kevlaar,
　　Take book and rosary,
And there, by our holy mother
　　Thy sick heart cured will be."

Now wave the church's banners,
　　Now sounds the church's song ;
On the Rhine, in Cologne, the holy
　　Procession moves along.

The mother follows the pilgrims,
  Her son she leadeth now ;
And both join in the chorus :
  " Oh ! Mary, praised be thou ! "

.   .   .   .   .   .

### 2.

The holy mother in Kevlaar
  Is decked in her best array ;
She 's busy, for there are plenty
  Of sick to heal to-day.

The sick ones on her altar
  Lay gifts which they deem meet ;
There, waxen limbs they offer
  And waxen hands and feet.

And he who gives a wax-hand
  Feels in his own no pain,
And he who gives a wax-foot
  Feels his grow well again.

To Kevlaar went many on crutches,
  Who now can dance in the air ;
And many now play the fiddle
  Who had no sound finger there.

The mother took a wax-light
  And formed of it a heart :
" Take that to the holy mother,
  She 'll cure thy deepest smart."


The son took, sighing, the wax-heart,
  To the image he stepped, with a sigh,
These words from his heart come streaming,
  As the tear-drops stream from his eye :


" Thou holy one, most blessèd,
  Thou purest, God-like maid,
Before thee, queen of heaven,
  My sorrows shall be laid.


" With mother I was living
  In the city called Cologne,
A town that has many hundreds
  Of chapels and churches of stone.


" Next door to us lived Gretchen,
  But dead, alas ! is she !
Oh ! Mary, I bring thee a wax-heart,
  Heal *my* heart's misery.

" Do thou my sick heart comfort,
  And morn and night I 'll bow
In prayer, and sing devoutly :
  " Oh ! Mary, praised be thou."

.    .    .    .    .    .

### 3.

The sick son and his mother
  In their little chamber slept ;
The holy mother then entered
  And softly to them stepped.

Low over the sick youth bending,
  She stopped—and her hand did lay
Upon his sore heart gently,—
  Then smiled, and passed away.

All this, and more, the mother
  Saw as she lay asleep ;
The dog barked loud and woke her
  Out of her slumbers deep.

And there, outstretched, was lying
  Her son,—and he was dead ;
On his visage pale was shining
  The early morning-red.

Her hands the mother folded,—
 She felt—she knew not how ;
She sang low and devoutly :
 "Oh ! Mary, praised be thou."

# The Hartz Journey.

## DIE HARZREISE.

---

## On the Mountain Stands the Cottage.

### AUF DEM BERGE STEHT DIE HÜTTE.

ON the mountain stands the cottage
    Where the ancient miner lives,
There the green old fir-tree rustles,
    Golden light the moon there gives.

In the cottage, carved most richly,
    Stands an arm-chair, quaint and high ;
He that sits there, he is happy
    And that happy one am I.

On the footstool sits the maiden,
    With her arm propped on my knee ;
Eyes that two blue stars resemble
    And a rose-red mouth has she.

And the dear, blue stars then open
   Heaven-wide to gaze at me,
And she lays her lily-finger
   On her rose-lips, playfully.


" No, the mother does not see us,
   For she spins unceasingly,
And the father plays the zither
   To the ancient melody."


And the maiden whispers softly,
   Softly, in a voice suppressed :—
Many an important secret
   Thus she poured into my breast—


" But since grandame's dead and buried
   We can nevermore repair
To the Schützenhof at Goslar,
   —And it is so lovely there.


" Here alas ! it is so lonely,
   On this mountain cold and steep,
And in winter we seem, truly,
   Buried in the snow-fall deep.

" And I am a timid maiden,
  Like unto a child, I fear
All the evil mountain-goblins
  That, at night, come prowling near."

Sudden stops the maid, affrighted
  By her voice, that sinks and dies ;
Both her little hands she raises
  Pressing them on both her eyes.

And the fir-tree rustles louder,
  And the spin-wheel creaks and hums,
And the zither's song, between them,
  In the old refrain still comes :

" Have no fear, thou lovely maiden,
  Of the evil spirits' power ;
For the angels, dearest maiden,
  Watch o'er thee at every hour !"

## The Shepherd Boy 's a Very King.

*KÖNIG IST DER HIRTENKNABE.*

THE shepherd boy 's a very king,
   His throne is on a verdant mound,
And with the sun above his head
   As with the heaviest gold he 's crowned.

The sheep are lying at his feet,
   With crosses red, soft flatterers they—
The calves, who are his Cavaliers,
   Are strutting proudly on their way.

The little goats his court-players are,
   And all the birds and all the kine
Try, with their flutes and little bells,
   To make the chamber-music fine.

And all this sweetly sounds and rings,
   And 'midst it all sweet rustlings creep,
Of spruce-trees and of waterfalls,
   Until the monarch sinks in sleep.

But in the meanwhile, there must reign
  The minister, and he is found
To be the dog, whose snarling bark
  Is heard in echoes all around.

"To govern is so very hard,"
  The young king murmurs drowsily,
"Oh! would that with my dearest queen,
  Already I at home might be.

"For in the arms of my sweet queen
  My royal head so softly lies,
And all my boundless kingdom is
  Contained within her lovely eyes."

## ¶ Am the Princess Ilse.

*ICH BIN DIE PRINZESSIN ILSE.*

I AM the Princess Ilse,
　　And Ilsenstein 's my home ;
That we two may taste love's rapture,
　　To my castle with me come.

And there I will anoint thee
　　With my waters clear and fair,
Thy pains shall be forgotten,
　　Thou comrade sick with care !

In my white arms will I fold thee,
　　And on my bosom white
There shalt thou lie a-dreaming
　　Of fairy-tales' delight.

I 'll fondle and I 'll kiss thee,
　　As I kissed and fondled, one day,
Belovèd Emperor Heinrich,
　　Who now has passed away.

The dead are gone forever,
  The living live with us ;
And I am fair and blooming,
  My heart laughs, tremulous.

And when my heart is laughing,
  My crystal palace rings out ;
Then dance the knights and maidens
  And jubilant vassals shout.

The silken trains then rustle,
  And clanking spurs are worn,
The dwarfs sound drum and trumpet
  And fiddle, and blow their horn.

But thou shalt lie enfolded,
  Like the Emperor, in my arm ;
I stopped his ears from hearing
  The trumpet's wild alarm.

# Northsea Cycle.

NORDSEE CYCLUS.

---

## Epilogue.

EPILOG.

A S in the field the stalks of wheat,
   Thus grow and sway man's thoughts
      Within his mind.
But the tender thoughts of poets
Are like gaily interspersed
      Red and blue flowers.

      Red and blue flowers !
The petulant reaper discards you as useless,
Wooden flails thresh you scornfully,
Even the destitute wanderer,
Whom a glimpse of you delights and refreshes,
      Shakes his head,
And calls you beautiful weeds.

But the rustic maiden,
The wreath-binder,
Adores you and plucks you,
And decks her lovely locks with you,
And thus adorned, she hies to the dancing-green
Where the sweet strains of pipe and fiddle resound,
Or to the quiet beech-tree
Where the voice of the belovèd sounds sweeter far
Than pipe and fiddle.

# New Spring.

## NEUER FRÜHLING.

———

## The Slender Water=Lily.

### DIE SCHLANKE WASSERLILIE.

THE slender water-lily
    Looks up from the lake in a dream :
The moon wafts brightly downward
    A loving, longing beam.

Abashed, the wee head sinketh
    And back to the waves is drawn ;
And there, at her feet, she findeth
    The comrade pale and forlorn.

## The Rose Is Fragrant—but Whether She Feeleth.

*DIE ROSE DUFTET—DOCH OB SIE EMPFINDET.*

THE rose is fragrant—but whether she feeleth
　　All that she exhales ; and whether again
The nightingale feels what through our soul stealeth
　　At the sound of her lovely, echoing strain:—

I know it not.　But truth, most trying,
　　Oft chafes our souls ; and e'en if we see
That the rose and nightingale both have been lying,
　　This lie—like some others—most fruitful may be !

## Because I Love Thee, I Must Leave Thee.

*WEIL ICH DICH LIEBE, MUSS ICH FLIEHEND.*

BECAUSE I love thee, I must leave thee !
    Oh ! be not wroth,—I shun thy face !
Thy visage bright and fair, believe me,
    Hath near my mournful one no place.

Because I love thee—grow uncomely
    My features sad, and waste away ;
Perhaps, ere long, thou 'lt find me homely—
    Oh ! be not wroth,—I will not stay !

## Gentle Chimes With Sweetest Ring.

*LEISE ZIEHT DURCH MEIN GEMÜTH.*

GENTLE chimes with sweetest ring
　　O'er my soul are stealing;
Ring out little song of spring,
　　Through the distance pealing.

To the cottage wing thy flight
　　Where bloom flowers tender ;
When a rose there greets thy sight,
　　Say my love I send her.

# There Was an Aged Monarch.

*ES WAR EIN ALTER KÖNIG.*

THERE was an aged monarch,
    Gray was his hair, sad was his life;
The poor old monarch married
    A fair and youthful wife.

There was a handsome page-boy,
    Gay was his heart, blonde was his hair;
The silken train he carried
    Of the queen so young and fair.

Know'st thou the olden story?
    It is so sweet, so sad to tell.
They both were doomed to perish,
    They loved each other too well,

# Miscellaneous.

## VERSCHIEDENE.

.

———

## SERAPHINE.

### I

## When ¶ Through the Dreamy Forest.

*WANDL' ICH IN DEM WALD DES ABENDS.*

WHEN I through the dreamy forest
 Wander on at eventide,
Ever does thy slender figure
 There go wand'ring by my side.

Are not these thy lovely features?
 Thy white veil that softly stirs?
Or is it the moonlight only
 Breaking thro' the gloomy firs?

Do I hear my own tears falling
 As they course down quietly?
Or dost thou walk weeping, dearest
 Verily, there next to me?

III

2

## On the Silent Shores of Ocean.

*AM DEM STILLEN MEERESSTRANDE.*

ON the silent shores of ocean
    Dusky night has fast been falling,
And the moon breaks thro' the cloudrifts,
    And the waves are softly calling :

" Is that fellow there demented,
    Or in love perhaps ?   For very
Merry, and yet sad he seemeth,
    Sad, and at the same time merry."

But the moon laughs out, and calleth
    Clearly, from her high position :
" He 's in love, and he 's demented,
    And a poet in addition ! "

### 3

# ¶ See a White Mew Yonder.

*DAS IST EINE WEISSE MÖWE.*

I SEE a white mew yonder,
　　Whose flutt'ring wings are spread
Above the darkling billows ;
　　The moon stands high o'erhead.

The shark and the roach are snapping
　　Out of their watery bed,
The mew is rising and falling ;
　　The moon stands high o'erhead.

Oh ! dear heart, ever restless,
　　Thou 'rt stirred with woe and dread !
The water is too near thee ;
　　The moon stands high o'erhead.
　　8

4

# ¶ Knew That Thou Dost Love Me.

*DAS DU MICH LIEBST, DAS WUSST' ICH.*

I KNEW that thou dost love me,
   'T was long ago made clear ;
But when thou did'st confess it,
   I thrilled with sudden fear.

'T is true, I climb'd the mountains,
   And sang exultingly ;
But, weeping, when the sun set,
   I walked beside the sea.

My heart the sun resembles,
   So flaming to the sight ;
And in love's endless ocean
   It setteth grand and bright.

5

## ইow Uonö'ringly tbe Sea=Mew.

*WIE NEUBEGIERIG DIE MÖWE.*

HOW wond'ringly the sea-mew
   Doth over at us peer,
Because I press so closely
   Unto thy lips mine ear !

She 's longing to discover
   To what thy lips give vent ;
If words indeed, or kisses
   Into mine ear thou 'st sent.

Could I myself but fathom
   What hisses thus into me !
Thy words are with thy kisses
   Commingled wondrously.

6

## She Fled from Me Like a Timid Doe.

*SIE FLOH VOR MIR WIE'N REH SO SCHEU.*

SHE fled from me like a timid doe,
    And with the doe's speed vying ;
She clambered up from crag to crag,
    Her hair in the wind was flying.

Where to the sea the cliff descends
    To catch her I succeeded,
And her coy heart I softened there,
    As with soft words I pleaded.

Up there as high as heav'n we sat,
    And with heav'n's bliss pervaded ;
Deep under us, in the dusky sea,
    The sunlight slowly faded.

Deep under us, the beauteous sun
    Sank in the dusky ocean ;
The waves with rapture o'er it swept,
    In turbulent commotion.

Oh ! do not weep !   The sun lies not
   Dead 'neath those billows flowing,
But in my heart has hid itself
   With all its fire glowing.

7

## Shadowy Love and Shadowy Kisses.

*SCHATTENKÜSSE—SCHATTENLIEBE.*

SHADOWY love and shadowy kisses,
  Shadowy life, so wondrous strange !
Little fool, think'st thou that this is
  Ever true, and will not change ?

Like a dream fades all we cherish'd,
  All we firmly hoped to keep ;
Memory from our hearts has perish'd,
  And our eyes,—they close in sleep.

## 8

## The Damsel Stood by the Ocean.

*DAS FRÄULEIN STAND AM MEERE.*

THE damsel stood by the ocean,—
  Sighed long and heavily ;
So sad 't was, to her notion,
  The setting sun to see.

Dear miss, pray cease your fretting,
  An old trick have we here,
Before us it is setting,
  And rises in our rear.

9

## My Ship, with Black Sails, Sails Along.

*MIT SCHWARZEN SEGELN SEGELT MEIN
SCHIFF.*

MY ship, with black sails, sails along
     Far o'er the raging sea ;
Thou know'st how sad I am,—and yet,
     So sorely grievest me.

Thy heart is fickle as the wind,
     And sways unsteadily ;
My ship, with black sails, sails along
     Far o'er the raging sea.

10

## how Shamefully Thou 'st Acted.

*WIE SCHÄNDLICH DU GEHANDELT.*

HOW shamefully thou 'st acted,
　　From all men I 've concealed it ;
But I have sailed out to the sea,
　　And to the fishes revealed it.

Thy name on dry land, only,
　　May still be thought untainted ;
But in the sea is everyone
　　With thy disgrace acquainted.

## II

## The Roaring Waves.

*ES ZIEHEN DIE BRAUSENDEN WELLEN.*

THE roaring waves are making
    Straight for the land ;
They 're swelling and they 're breaking
    Upon the sand.

They come in endless fashion,
    Great, vigorous ;
At last, burst into passion,—
    What helps it us ?

## 12

# The Runic Stone Juts Out From the Beach.

*ES RAGT IN'S MEER DER RUNENSTEIN.*

THE Runic stone juts out from the beach,
  There I sit, as my thoughts go roaming ;
The wild wind pipes, the sea-gulls screech,
  The billows are flowing and foaming.

On many fair girls and comrades kind
  Have I my love been bestowing ;—
Where have they gone ?  Wild pipes the wind,
  The billows are foaming and flowing.

13

## Tbe Sea Gleams Fortb Beneatb tbe Sun.

*DAS MEER ERSTRAHLT IM SONNENSCHEIN.*

THE sea gleams forth beneath the sun
    As if of gold 't were made.
When I am dead, my brothers,
    In the sea I 'd fain be laid.

I 've always loved the sea so well ;
    Its flow hath soothingly
So oft refreshed my spirit ;
    Good friends, indeed, were we.

# ANGÉLIQUE.

## On Both her Eyes My hand I pressed.

*ICH HALTE IHR DIE AUGEN ZU.*

ON both her eyes my hand I pressed
   As a kiss from her I won ;
And now she will not let me rest,
   But asks wherefore 't was done.

From evening late until sunrise
   She questions without rest :
" Why did you cover both my eyes,
   As your lips to mine you pressed ? "

The reason why, I do not tell,
   Myself, I cannot guess—
But both her eyes I cover well,
   And my lips to hers I press.

# KATHARINE.

## Long Was I Songless and Dejected.

*GESANGLOS WAR ICH UND BEKLOMMEN.*

L ONG was I songless and dejected,
But now my muse returns to me ;
Just as our tears come unexpected,
So come our songs, quite suddenly.

Once more I sing, in rhythmic measure,
Of love so great, and greater woe,
Of hearts that quarrel in displeasure,
Yet break, when far apart they go.

At times, methinks, I feel the flutter
Of German oak-leaves o'er my brow—
Of meetings too, they seem to mutter,—
But these are dreams—they vanish now.

Anon sweet strains with rapture fill me,
The German nightingale's old lay—
How tenderly the soft notes thrill me !—
But these are dreams—they die away.

Where are the roses that delighted
  My fond heart once ?—Long since was spent
Their bloom, alas !—Their shades benighted
  Still haunt my soul with ghostly scent.

# Poems of the Times.

## ZEITGEDICHTE.

------

## Night Thoughts.

### NACHTGEDANKEN.

AT night I think of Germany,
And then all slumber flies from me ;
I can no longer close mine eyes,
The hot and bitter tears will rise.

The years pass close upon each other ;
And since I last beheld my mother,
Full twelve long years have come and gone,
And ever has my yearning grown.

My wistful yearning e'er has grown,
For o'er my soul a spell she 's thrown ;
From her my thoughts I cannot sever,
The dear old dame—God bless her ever !

She loves me well, the dear old dame,
   And in the lines that from her came,
'T is proven by the words all blurred
   How deep her mother's heart was stirred.

My mother 's in my mind alway ;
   Full twelve long years have passed away,
Full twelve long years have joined the past
   Since to my heart I clasped her last.

Oh ! Germany will ever stand !
   It is a strong and healthy land,
And with its oak, and linden trees
   I 'm sure to find it, when I please.

I should not thirst for Germany so,
   Did I not there my mother know ;
The fatherland will ever stay,—
   The mother may be called away.

Since I have left my native land,
   On many Death has laid its hand ;
I loved them once—I call the roll
   And count them now with bleeding soul.

Count them I must ; yet, as I count,
  Still higher does my torture mount,
As if the corpses, one by one,
  Climbed on my breast !—Thank God, they 're
    gone !

Thank God ! now, through my window, glance
  The cheerful morning rays of France.
My wife comes with Aurora's bloom
  To smile away the German gloom !

## Germany.

### DEUTSCHLAND.

GERMANIA'S fame will I extol,
  Oh ! hearken to my finest verse.
Yet high and higher soars my soul,
  And purest joys my heart traverse.

Before me lies the Book of Life :
  The many changes earth did see,
'Twixt good and bad the constant strife,—
  All this is now made clear to me.

From distant Frankish land once came
  Hell's darkest spirits, shrewd and sly,
Who brought disgrace and direst shame
  On pious, good old Germany.

Of all belief and virtue fair,
  Of all our faith in heav'nly gain,
Of all our good they laid us bare,—
  And gave us naught but sin and pain.

Oh ! then did German sunlight pale !
   It will not shine on German shame ;
And hollow sounds of funeral wail,
   Out of the German oak-trees came.


But suddenly the sun grew bright ;
   The oak-tree waves a joyous strain ;
There come the judges of the right,
   Avenging all our shame and pain.


The altars of deceit now shake,
   And fall into the seething broil,
All German hearts to thanks awake,—
   Now free is sacred German soil !


" See'st on the hills the flames shoot high ?
   Oh ! say, why sweeps the fire along ?"
" Those flames so fierce exemplify
   Germania's image, pure and strong."


Released from evil's sinful yoke,
   Now, all unharmed, stands Germany ;
And still the gloomy spot doth smoke,
   From which the lovelier form rose free.

The ancient oak-stems now unfold
   Their blossoms new, and wondrous sweet ;
Strange blossoms fade, and rustlings old
   Familiarly the senses greet.


Now all that 's lovely comes anew,
   All good returns without alloy,
And every German, staunch and true,
   Most gladly hails his German joy.


The olden virtues, olden ways,
   The hero's courage, old and good,
The German youth his sword now sways,
   For Hermann's grandson fears no blood.


A hero never breeds a dove ;—
   Most lion-like is Hermann's air,
But firm belief and trust in God
   Should equally with courage pair.


Their sorrows taught the German how
   Christ's lessons should be understood ;
All Germans are close brothers now,—
   Humanity alone is good.

Once more is heard the ancient lyre,
　With minstrel's song again we 're blest ;
Oh ! gentle muse, thou dost attire
　In lovely garb the hero's breast.


Against the French he went to war,
　And waged a hot and bitter fight ;
Their false oaths to avenge he swore,
　Dispensing death with bloody might.


At home our German women rose
　To soothe, with soft hands, bitter need,
And bind the sacred wounds of those
　Who for the Fatherland did bleed.


In festive garb—though black her dress—
　The lovely German woman beams,
Rare gems and flow'rs her form caress,
　Her belt of diamonds brightly gleams.


But lovelier, by far, is she,
　Methinks, when low I see her bend
Down o'er the sick-bed, lovingly,
　And there her soothing cares extend.

For, angel-like doth she appear
   With soothing draught, so tenderly
The wounded warrior's death to cheer,—
   Whose parting glance smiles gratefully.

To earn a hero's place of rest
   On battle-ground,—ah, that is sweet !
To breathe one's last on woman's breast,—
   For gods such Paradise is meet.

Alas ! you poor, poor sons of France,
   On you Dame Fortune does not smile !
For, on the Seine, the fair one's glance
   Did covet but your gold so vile.

Oh ! German women, German women !
   These words enfold a magic charm
Oh ! German women, German women,
   May time preserve you from all harm !

# New Songs.

---

## A Woman.

*EIN WEIB.*

THEY loved each other past belief ;
  A rogue was she, and he a thief ;
And when his crimes he went about,
  She laughed—full on her bed stretched out.

The days went by in joy and play,
  At night upon his breast she lay,
And when to jail they led him out,
  From the window came her merry shout.

He sent her word " Oh, come to me,
  So greatly do I long for thee,
I call on thee, I pine for thee "—
  She shook her head, still laughingly.

137

They hanged him up at six in the morn,
　　At seven he lay in his grave forlorn ;
But she—at eight already quaffed
　　Her purple wine, and gaily laughed.

# Spring's Festival.

## FRÜHLINGSFEIER.

WITH such sad bliss doth Spring delude !
  The blooming maids, the savage flocks,
  Onward they storm, with flying locks
And cries of pain, and bosoms nude:—
    " Adonis ! Adonis ! "

The night descends.  The torchlight gleams,
  As to and fro they scour the wood,
  Which echoes to their frenzied mood,
Their cries and laughter, sobs and screams:—
    " Adonis ! Adonis ! "

The lovely youth, surpassing fair,
  Stretched on the ground lies pale and dead,
  His blood dyes all the flowers red,
And sounds of wailing fill the air:—
    " Adonis ! Adonis ! "

## What I have, Ask Not, My Darling.

*FRAG' NICHT, LIEBCHEN, WAS ICH HABE.*

WHAT I have, ask not, my darling,
  Ask me rather what I am ;
For I have no mighty treasures,
  Yet both good and true I am.

Ask me not just how my life 's spent,
  But for whom—that ask of me ;
For my life is poor and lonely,
  But my life is spent for thee.

Ask me not what are my pleasures,
  Ask me not what is my pain ;
For by joy is he deserted
  Whose poor heart is rent in twain.

# The Lesson.

*DIE LEHRE.*

MOTHER to little bee :
    " Candle-light shun," says she ;
But to these words, indeed,
    Little bee pays no heed.

Near the light does he come,
    Singing his hum-hum-hum,—
Mother's cry hears not he :
    " Little bee, little bee."

Young blood has lost its head,
    Darts in the flame so red ;
Into the flame darts he,
    " Little bee, little bee."

Flame bursts out flaringly,
    Dealing death glaringly !
" Maidens wee must thou shun,
    Little son, little son ! ".

# GOETHE.

# Poems.

*GEDICHTE.*

--------

## The Wand'rer's Night Song.

*DES WAND'RER'S NACHTLIED.*

ON every hill
All is still ;
Scarce a breeze
Stirs the trees'
Topmost nest.
The birds, in the woods, hush their song.
Wait, thou too, ere long,
Wilt have rest.

## Ocean Calm.

*MEERESSTILLE.*

IN the water reigns deep silence,
　　Without motion broods the sea,
On its smooth expanse the sailor
　　Rests his glances anxiously.
Not a breeze from any quarter,—
　　Awful stillness of the grave.
Thro' the boundless space of water
　　Nowhere, nowhere stirs a wave.

## ḣappɒ Voɒage.

*GLÜCKLICHE FAHRT.*

THE mists are dispersing,
   Serene are the heavens,
And Æolus loosens
   The anxious band.
Fresh breezes now flurry,
   The sailor bestirs him ;
Oh, hurry ! oh, hurry !
   The billows part lightly,
The distance approacheth,—
   Lo ! there is the land !

## Swiss Song.

*SCHWEIZERLIED.*

ON a hill-top
   Was I sitting,
And the birdies
   Watched I;
They were singing,
   They were springing,
Nest-building
   On high.

In a garden
   Was I standing,
Watched the busy
   Bees swarm ;
Buzzing, humming,
   Quickly coming,
Their cells there
   To form.

To a meadow
  Then I wander'd,
Watched the butter-
  Flies play ;
Sipping sweetly,
  Rising fleetly,
Oh ! so pretty
  Were they.


And now up comes
  My Hansel ;
To him, gladly,
  I show
How 't was done, then,—
  And in fun, then,
We do it
  Just so.

# The Angler.

## *DER FISCHER.*

THE water surged, the water swelled,
    An angler sat on the shore ;
Gazed calmly at the rod he held,
    His heart cool to the core.
And as he sits and as he lists,
    The flood uplifts and parts,
And then out from the surging mists
    A wat'ry maiden starts.


She spoke to him, she sang to him :
    " Why lure my brood on high,
With human wit and human wiles,
    Where in the glare they die?
Oh ! if thou knew'st how cosily
    Here, the little fishes dwell,
Thou would'st come down, as thou art, to me,
    And then thou would'st grow well.

" Is not the moon, the dear sun too,
  Soothed by the ocean's flow?
As wave on wave they breathe anew,
  Do they not lovelier grow?
Does not the sky's deep glow tempt thee,
  Its moist, translucent blue?
Would'st not thy own face mirrored see,
  Here, in eternal dew?"


The water surged, the water swelled,
  Wet his bare foot above;
His soul yearned forth, as tho' impelled
  By greetings from his love!
She spoke to him, she sang to him,
  —Then all with him was o'er—
Half drew she him, half yielded he,—
  And then was seen no more.

## Vanitas Vanitatum.

ON nothing have I set my heart,
　　　　Heyday !
Thus so much good doth life impart,
　　　　Heyday !
And he who would my comrade be,
Must glasses clink, sing merrily,
And drain this wine with me.
　　．

On gold and gain my heart set I,
　　　　Heyday !
But joy and mirth I lost thereby,
　　　　Lackaday !
The coin went rolling all around,
If in one spot I thought 't was found,
To another it would bound !
　　　　　　　．

I set my heart on women, next,
　　　　Heyday !
But grievously was I then vex'd,
　　　　Lackaday !

The false one other lovers sought,
The true one was a bore, methought,
The best could not be bought.


I set my heart on travels wide,
          Heyday !
Far from my native land I hied,
          Lackaday !
And things to me seemed nowhere right,
Strange fare by day, hard bed by night,
None understood me quite.


I set my heart on honor and fame,
          Heyday !
Lo ! others soon won more of a name,
          Lackaday !
When I at last had risen high,
All folks looked then on me awry,
None could I satisfy.


I set my heart on fray and fight,
          Heyday !
And many a battle we won outright,
          Heyday !

To hostile lands did we repair,
Our friends were doom'd no better to fare,
And I a leg lost there.

Now I 've set my heart on naught, you see,
                    Heyday !
And all the world belongs to me !
                    Heyday !
Our song and feasting all must stop ;
Now all this wine, let 's drink it up,
Out with the very last drop !

# GEIBEL.

155

# Poems.

## GEDICHTE.

---

## O Therefore Is the Spring so Bright.

*O DARUM IST DER LENZ SO SCHÖN.*

O THEREFORE is the Spring so bright
   With music, flow'rs, and sun,
Because o'er dale and mountain height
   Its song must soon pass on.

And therefore does love's ecstasy
   Such blissful dreams inspire,
Because like blossoms on the tree
   They languish and expire.

And yet, they leave so warm a glow,
   Such wealth our hearts to bless !
Sweet love, high rapture did I know,
   E'en that is happiness !

Throughout the scanty day my breast
  Drank in each golden ray ;
The glorious sun has sunk to rest,
  And now let come what may.

If blessings new, if bitter woe,
  I will accept it all ;
The treasure in my heart below
  Is mine, whate'er befall !

# The Poor Good=for=Nothing.

*DER ARME TAUGENICHTS.*

IT, verily, is not my fault
    That my poor nose is all awry,
And that at the tavern 't is easier to halt
    Than to work at the plough, in the fields near by ;
And that for the miller's child I care
    Much more than for our portly priest !
But I waste my breath—this bad world ne'er
    Can understand me in the least !

The miller's a grim old fellow, forsooth !
    A good-for-nothing he says, am I :
And the village-folk all take this for truth,
    And his rosy daughter joins in the cry !
At the mill-brook she spies me, and pulls a long face,
    And turns up her dear little nose in disdain,
Contriving to do this with so much grace
    That with anger and love my heart bursts in
        twain !

Now out to the trees my sorrow I bring,
  But they are so mute, but they are so cool ;
The cuckoo and bullfinch mockingly sing
  And the beetles are buzzing : Thou fool, thou
    fool !
If this goes on, if things soon don't mend,
  Then here in the village, I 'll stand it no more,
Across the big forest my footsteps I 'll wend,
  And fiddle my way then from door to door !

# In April.

*IM APRIL.*

OH, dewey eve in spring-time,
How fond of thee am I !
The sky with clouds is curtain'd,
A few stars gleam on high.

What seems like love's soft breathing
The balmy air exhales ;
The violet's sweet perfume
Ascends from all the dales.

A song just like this evening
I fain would waft aloft ;
But I find none that soundeth
So dark, so mild and soft.

# O Still This Ardent Yearning!

*O STILLE DIES VERLANGEN !*

O STILL this ardent yearning,
　　Soothe this sweet agony !
To clasp thee I am burning,
　　Let thy lover come to thee !
E'en now the world lies dreaming,
　　Night sheds its fragrant dew ;
The moon, from her blue vault beaming,
　　Keeps watch o'er lovers true.
On those with fond love burning
　　She beams most tenderly.
O still this ardent yearning,
　　Let thy lover come to thee !


Like fire that sweetly consumes me,
　　Thou glowest in my heart ;
O lift the veil that dooms me
　　From thee to keep apart !

To thy red lips let me cling then
  And drink thy soul divine,
My own soul I will bring then
  And yield it up for thine—
O still this ardent yearning,
  Soothe this sweet agony !
To clasp thee I am burning,
  Let thy lover come to thee !


The golden stars send greeting
  Down from the heavens bright :
Kisses and whispers are fleeting
  Mysterious, through the night.
And even the little flowers
  Their heads with longing move,
The nightingales sing in the bowers ;
  Thou, too, may'st dream and love !
O still this ardent yearning,
  Let thy lover come to thee !
In dreams with passion burning
  We two shall blessèd be.

## Gondoliera.

*GONDOLIERA.*

O COME to me when thro' the night
　　The starry legions ride !
Then o'er the sea, in the moonshine bright,
　Our gondola will glide.
The air is soft as a lover's jest,
　And gently gleams the light,
The zither sounds, and thy soul is blest
　To join in this delight.
O come to me when thro' the night
　The starry legions ride !
Then o'er the sea, in the moonshine bright
　Our gondola will glide.

This is the hour for lovers true,
　Darling, like thee and me ;
Serenely smile the heavens blue
　And calmly sleeps the sea.

And as it sleeps, a glance will say
    What speech in vain has tried ;
The lips then do not shrink away,
    Nor is a kiss denied.
O come to me when thro' the night
    The starry legions ride !
Then o'er the sea, in the moonshine bright
    Our gondola will glide.

# Let No One Ask Me Ever.

*WOLLE KEINER MICH FRAGEN.*

LET no one ask me ever
   Why beats my heart so high,
For I, myself, can never
   Tell the reason why.

My dizzy brain is reeling,
   And dream-like all has grown ;
My every thought and feeling
   Is thine alone.

Since first thine eyes did bless me,
   I 'm lost to time and space ;
To my heart I fain would press thee
   And die in thine embrace.

My life—I 'd gladly give it,
   For a single smile from thee,
And thou—must I believe it ?—
   Deniest it me !

Is 't fate, or thy own will, dear,
   That blind to me thou art?
Now weep I here, quite still, dear,
   Till breaks my heart.

## Girlhood's Songs.

*MÄDCHENLIEDER.*

### I.

THE pinks that I so cherish,
　　Each with its purple star,—
Now all of them must perish,
　　For thou art far !


The flames once gladly tended
　　Upon my hearth, now are
In smoke and ashes ended,
　　For thou art far !


Life's joys no longer win me,
　　I see nor flower, nor star ;
My heart is dead within me
　　For thou art far !

## II.

HOW bright the sun was beaming,
The trees all blossom'd in May,
Thine eyes with love were gleaming—
That 's passed away !

Long since the buds have perished,
For Autumn's work was swift ;
The blissful dreams I cherish'd,—
In the wind they drift !

## Answer.

*ANTWORT.*

YOU ask me why, dear maiden,
My songs with tears are laden?
What grieves me must I say?
My spring has passed untasted,
My youth in dreams been wasted,
My love been trifled away.

Life's cup swelled higher and higher,
To drink I lacked desire,—
I let the cup pass on;
Figs, grapes, from green vines pending,
With sweet pomegranates blending,
Lured me,—I would have none!

As evening then came stealing,
The glorious sun concealing,
My thirst awoke at last;
But then the cup had vanish'd,
The luscious fruits were banish'd,
And night was falling fast.

Now, by the world forsaken,
Out to the streets I 've taken
  My sorrow's piteous lay :
My spring has passed untasted
My youth in dreams been wasted,
  My love been trifled away.

## As It Will Happen.

*WIE ES GEHT.*

" HE loves thee not ! He trifles but with thee !"
    They said to her, and then she bowed her
      head,
And pearly tears, like roses' dew, wept she.
    Oh ! that she ever trusted what they said !
For when he came and found his bride in doubt,
    Then, from sheer spite, he would not show his
      sorrow ;
He played and drank and laughed, day in day out,—
    To weep from night until the morrow !

'T is true, an angel whispered in her heart :
    " He 's faithful still, Oh ! lay thy hand in his " :
And he, too, felt 'midst grief and bitter smart :
    " She loves thee ! After all, thy love she is ;
Let but a gentle word pass on each side,
    The spell that parts you now, will then be broken !"
They came—each looked on each—Oh ! evil pride !—
    That single word remained unspoken !

They parted then.   As in a church one oft
    Extinguished sees the altar lamps' red fires,
Their light grows dim, then once more flares aloft
    In radiance bright—and thereupon expires,—
So died their love ; at first lamented o'er,
    Then yearned for ardently, and  then—forgotten,
Until the thought that they had loved before,
    Of mere delusion seemed begotten !

But sometimes, when the moon shone out at night,
    Each started from his couch ! Ah, was it not
Bedewed with tears? And tears, too, dimmed their
        sight,
    Because these two had dreamed—I know not
        what !
And then the dear old times woke in their heart,
    Their foolish doubts, their parting, that had driven
Their souls so far, so very far apart,—
    Oh ! God, let both now be forgiven !

# See'st Thou the Sea?

*SIEH'ST DU DAS MEER?*

SEE'ST thou the sea? The sun gleams on its wave
        With splendor bright ;
But where the pearl lies buried in its cave
        Is deepest night.

The sea am I.   My soul, in billows bold,
        Rolls fierce and strong ;
And over all, like to the sunlight's gold,
        There streams my song.

It throbs with love and pain as though possess'd
        Of magic art,
And yet, in silence bleeds, within my breast,
        My gloomy heart.

# Separation, Desolation.

## *SCHEIDEN, LEIDEN.*

THOUGH thou art gone, though thou art far
  And angry still with me,
Yet my thoughts, full of sadness, are
  All day and night with thee.
They dwell upon thy dear blue eyes
  And on thy heart divine—
Oh, no one shall I ever find
  Whose love can be like thine !


The world stood wreathed in flowers bright
  While yet I was with thee ;
The tree-tops rustled from each height,
  The moon beamed tenderly.
Thou culled'st a rose, I kissed thee then
  And sang as thy lips touched mine ;
Oh, no one shall I ever find
  Whose love can be like thine.

'T is true, I 'm free as the falcon bold
  That skyward wings his flight,
And who this fair world may behold
  All bathed in golden light ;
But he has a cosy nest,—and where
  Shall I, some day, recline ?
Oh, no one shall I ever find
  Whose love can be like thine !

Oh, bitter hour, oh, bitter day
  That tore us two apart !
Since then all joy has fled away
  And peace has left my heart.
Now I may roam o'er land and sea
  But rest will ne'er be mine ;
Oh, no one shall I ever find
  Whose love can be like thine !

## Onward.

### *VORWÄRTS.*

CEASE thy dreaming !   Cease thy quailing !
   Wander on untiringly.
Though thy strength may all seem failing,
   Onward ! must thy watchword be.

Durst not tarry, tho' life's roses
   'Round about thy footsteps throng,
Tho' the ocean's depth discloses
   Sirens, with their witching song.

Onward ! onward ! ever calling
   On thy muse, in life's stern fray,
Till thy fever'd brow feels falling
   From above, a golden ray.

Till the verdant wreath, victorious,
   Crown with soothing shade thy brow ;
Till the spirit's flames rise glorious
   Over thee, with sacred glow.

Onward then, through hostile fire,
Onward thro' death's agony !
Who to heaven would aspire,
Must a valiant warrior be.

# Hope.

*HOFFNUNG.*

LET Winter threaten as it will,
  And with fierce mien distress thee,
Though snow and ice he scatter,—still
  Spring *must* return to bless thee.

What tho' dense mists, in mountain-piles,
  The sun's rays now hold captured,
One of these days, beneath its smiles,
  The world will wake, enraptured.

Blow on, ye storms !   Blow on with might,
  I know no timorous feeling ;
For after all, Spring, over night,
  Will come, on tiptoe stealing.

All clad in green then wakes the earth,
  What happened, she 'd fain discover ;
She laughs to the sunny heavens in mirth,
  With bliss she is brimming over,

She twines gay wreaths, which in her hair,
   With roses and wheat she is tressing,
Bids the brooks flow clear, as tho' they were
   Bright tears, born of a blessing.

Therefore, be still !   Oh, yield not, heart,
   Midst ice and cold to sadness !
For all the world there 's set apart
   A grand may-day of gladness.

Though often Hell on earth seem nigh,
   And darkest fears oppress thee,
Trust dauntlessly in God on high,—
   Spring *must* return to bless thee.

# Songs.

## *LIEDER.*

---

## Let tbe Songs I 'm Singing Golden Bridges Be.

### *GOLDNE BRÜCKEN SEIEN ALLE LIEDER MIR*

LET the songs I 'm singing
  Golden bridges be,
That my love may wander
  O'er them, pet, to thee.

And on dream's swift pinions,
  In sorrow or delight—
Oh ! let me be carried
  To thy heart each night.

## The Silent Water=Lily.

*DIE STILLE WASSERROSE.*

THE silent  water-lily
　　From the blue lake rises up,
Her moistened leaves are trembling,
　　And snow white is her cup.

And then the moon from heaven,
　　Its golden radiance all,
And all its beams refulgent
　　Into her lap lets fall.

In the lake, about the flower,
　　A white swan circles 'round ;
It sings so soft, so sweetly,
　　On the flow'r its gaze is bound.

It sings so soft, so sweetly,
　　And, singing, would die away—
O flower, snow-white flower,
　　What the song means, can'st thou say ?

# A Crown of Cornflow'rs Let Me Wreathe.

*KORNBLUMEN FLECHT' ICH DIR ZUM KRANZ.*

A CROWN of cornflow'rs let me wreathe
   And in thy blonde locks twine ;
How clearly on the gold beneath
   Their glossy blue doth shine !

That blue crown is a joy to me,
   It tells me ever anew,
That none, my child, can be like thee,
   So tender and so true.

And then, its blue, like heav'n above,
   In sweet wise whispers this :
That I have found in thy dear love
   A Paradise of bliss !

# Within a Rosebush Love Once Sat.

*DIE LIEBE SASS ALS NACHTIGALL.*

WITHIN a rosebush Love once sat
　　As nightingale, and sang
Such wondrous lovely music that
　　The wood with echoes rang.

And at the sound there rose aloft
　　A thousand perfumes rare,
And all the tree-tops rustled soft,
　　And softly stirred the air.

Hush'd were the brooks whose merry bound
　　Had just come from the hill ;
The little does, to catch the sound,
　　As in a dream stood still.

And, over all, the sunlight streamed
　　And ever grew more bright ;
Ravine and wood and flowers seemed
　　All bathed in crimson light.

I also caught that music when
   Thro' the woods I strolled along, —
Oh ! all that I have sung since then
   Was the echo of that song !

## Once Bowed with Grief and Sore Distress'd.

*WOHL LAG ICH EINST IN GRAM UND SCHMERZ.*

ONCE bowed with grief and sore distress'd
　　I wept all day and night ;
And now I weep because my breast
　　O'erflows with pure delight.

Methinks my bosom doth contain
　　The heavens wide and far ;
Oh, greatest bliss, oh, greatest pain,
　　How much alike you are !

# At Last the Daylight Fadeth.

*NUN IST DER TAG GESCHIEDEN.*

A T last the daylight fadeth
   With all its noise and glare,
Refreshing peace pervadeth
   The darkness everywhere.

On the fields deep silence hovers ;
   The woods now wake alone ;
What daylight ne'er discovers
   Their songs to the night make known.

And what, when the sun is shining,
   I ne'er can tell to thee,
To whisper it now I am pining,—
   Oh ! come and hearken to me !

## When Evening's Dying Flames Sink Yonder.

### WENN STILL MIT SEINEN LETZTEN FLAMMEN.

WHEN evening's dying flames sink yonder
　　Into the waters, silently,
Beneath the beeches then we wander,
　　Where slopes the forest to the sea.

We see the moon thro' cloud-rifts sailing,
　　We hear the distant nightingale ;
We breathe sweet scents—but words are failing,
　　For, what can empty speech avail ?

No songs can tell our greatest rapture,
　　The heart is quiet when most blest :
A kiss to win, a glance to capture,—
　　And every longing is at rest !

# Thou Askest Me, My Gold=haired Pet.

*DU FRAGST MICH, DU, MEIN BLONDES LIEB.*

THOU askest me, my gold-haired pet
  Wherefore my lips ne'er part ?
Because love is abiding,
  In secret abiding,
  Within my heart.


Can fire soar upwards, singing,
When it toward heaven will ?
It spreads its pinions high and red,
  So high and red,
  And yet so still.


And even the rose is silent
When opening to the light ;
It glows and blooms, but says no word,
  But says no word
  Thro' the summer night.

Such is my love since ever
'T was kindly met by thee ;
It glows and throbs within me,
   Deep within me,
   But speechlessly.

# A Thousand Kisses, Ere We Part.

*VIEL TAUSEND, TAUSEND, KÜSSE GIEB.*

A THOUSAND kisses, ere we part,
  Oh, give me, love, I pray thee !
A thousand kisses then, sweetheart,
  With rapture I 'll repay thee.

This earth of ours is far too great,
  With hills and seas unending !
Two faithful hearts they separate
  Whose lives might well be blending.

As a little bird I 'd fain take flight,
  And then the breezes might carry
Me far out in the moonlit night,
  With my gold-haired pet to tarry.

And if I found her bow'd in gloom,
  Then I would share her sadness ;
But were my rosebud bright with bloom,
  How I would trill with gladness !

How, on the peaceful night, that sound
  Should go forth, sweetly ringing !
No nightingale could e'er be found
  With more delicious singing.

A thousand kisses, ere we part,
  Oh, give me, love, I pray thee !
A thousand kisses, then, sweetheart,
  With rapture I 'll repay thee.

# The Time of Roses Now has Fled.

*VORÜBER IST DIE ROSENZEIT.*

THE time of roses now has fled,
  The lilies now are here ;
But high above them all are spread
  The heavens blue and clear.


O rapture fraught with woe, farewell !
  O brief love, thou may'st go !
Within my heart there still doth dwell
  A calm and peaceful glow.


And since both joy and pain have sped
  Fair doth the world appear ;
The time of roses now has fled,
  The lilies now are here.

# Now May Is Upon Us.

*DER MAI IST GEKOMMEN.*

NOW May is upon us, the blossoms all have come,
  Let those who so please with their cares stay
    at home !
As the clouds sail forth, in the heaven's unfurl'd,
So I would also wander into the wide, wide world !

Dear father, dear mother, God's blessings on ye !
Who knows what the future in store has for me !
There 's many a good road that I never yet did
    stride,
There 's many a good wine that I never yet have
    tried.

Then up and away, thro' sunshine bright away !
Far over the mountains and where deep valleys lay !
The brooks all are singing and softly waves each
    tree,
My heart like a lark is and joineth in the glee.

In the village, at evening, I enter all athirst :
Mine host, mine host, bring a jug of good wine
    first,
And thou, jolly fiddler, come fiddle me a song,
And a tune about my sweetheart I 'll sing thee along.


But if I find no shelter at night, I shall sleep
'Neath heaven's blue cover, the stars a watch will
    keep ;
The trees, in the breeze, will lull me tenderly,
At dawn, the sunlight's kiss will gently waken me.


Oh ! roaming, Oh ! roaming, thou merry swain's
    delight !
God's breath thro' my bosom sweeps fresh from the
    height !
Then sings and exults towards heaven my heart,—
And Oh ! thou wide wide world, how beautiful thou
    art !

# The Lilies Glow Forth Sweetly.

*DIE LILIEN GLÜHN IN DÜFTEN.*

THE lilies glow forth sweetly,
　From the trees the blossoms sway,
On the still air rises, fleetly,
　My dream, in bright array.

And 'neath its glance, the flowers
　All bow their heads,—and the sigh
Of the trees, and the birds in the bowers,
　Are hushed as it passes by.

How doth this nightly hour
　My heart with rest imbue !
My will has lost its power,
　The old love stirs anew !

Methinks the heav'ns are giving
　Their greeting unto me !
With God and all that's living
　I fain at peace would be !

# As in the Sky Appears the Sun.

*DIE SONN' HEBT AN VOM WOLKENZELT.*

AS in the sky appears the sun,
  With furtive radiance glowing,
Thro' woods and meadows there doth run
  A trickling, purling, flowing.

The ice dissolves, then melts the snow,
  Soon tender buds come peeping :
" Ye violets," sing breezes low,
  " Wake, wake, now, from your sleeping."

Oh ! gentle stirrings in the vales !
  Oh ! Spring's sweet exhalation !
My bosom, too, the song exhales
  That rings through all creation !

And as the air, in wondrous wise,
  Grows e'er more blue before me,
Strange yearnings in my soul arise,—
  I know not what 's come o'er me !

My breast grows wide, as though e'en now
　　New germs were upward striving !
Art come back, youth ? Oh ! love, art thou
　　Once more in me reviving ?

# Oh, hurry My Steed.

*O SCHNELLER MEIN ROSS.*

OH ! hurry my steed, be fleet, be fleet,
  How idly thy steps seem to tarry ;
To the woods, to the woods, my burden sweet,
  My blissful secret to carry.

On the hills, a red voluptuous glow
  The evening sun is flinging ;
The birds who gladness, too, would know
  From every branch are singing.

Oh ! if to soar like the lark on high
  To me the power were given,
My great, great happiness would I
  Proclaim to the radiant heaven.

Or could I on the storm god's wings
  To the dark blue ocean hurry,
What deep in my bosom throbs and rings,
  'Neath the silent waves I 'd bury.

No human ear shall hear my song !
  On high like the lark, I can't flutter,
Like the storm I cannot scurry along,
  And yet—my secret must utter.

Then learn it, ye beeches, in yon gorge at rest !
  Learn it, moon, that blinks from yon river !
She is mine ! She is mine ! My lips most blest
  With her burning kisses still quiver.

# I Cannot Fathom Why.

*ICH WEISS NICHT WIE'S GESCHIEHT.*

I CANNOT fathom why,
  Whate'er my heart may sing,
Its songs incessantly
  With love's soft accents ring.

Nor why of love's delight
  I ne'er can silent be,
Though from its heaven bright
  They long since banished me.

My heart then scarce can say :
  Is joy to come again?
Or does youth's bygone day
  Re-echo in my strain ?

# New Sonnets.

*NEUE SONNETTEN.*

---

## Whene'er Two Hearts Must Sever.

*WENN ZICH ZWEI HERZEN SCHEIDEN.*

WHENE'ER two hearts must sever,
   In which love once has dwelt,
'T is a mighty grief,—and never
   Could mightier be felt.
How sad it sounds when one must say :
" Farewell, farewell forever and aye ! "
Whene'er two hearts must sever,
   In which love once has dwelt.

When first the thought came o'er me
   That love might pass away,
I felt the sun before me
   Grow dark in the noon of day.

My ear then echoed in wondrous way :
" Farewell, farewell forever and aye ! "
When first the thought came o'er me
   That love might pass away !

My springtime all has vanished,
   The cause I well divine ;
For smiles and speech are banished
   From lips that once kissed mine.
A single clear word uttered they :
   " Farewell, farewell forever and aye ! "
My springtime all has vanished
   The cause I well divine.

# Oh! Touch It Not!

*O RÜHRET NICHT DARAN.*

WHENE'ER a heart with still love glows,
   Oh, touch it not ! and oh, take heed
Not to destroy the spark divine !
  It were not wisely done indeed.

If anywhere upon this earth
  A sacred little spot there be,
It is a youthful human heart
  That burns with first love piously.

Oh ! grudge it not this dream of spring,
  All wreathed about with blossoms fair !
You know not what a Paradise
  Would, with this dream, be lost fore'er.

How many a strong heart had to break
  That rudely from its love was torn !
How many a patient one has turned,
  And thenceforth harbored hate and scorn !

And some, still bleeding inwardly,
  Cried out for new joys in their pain,
And flung themselves into the mire—
  The beauteous God in them was slain.

Then would you weep and blame yourselves ;
  But rueful tears will never make
A withered rosebud bloom again,
  Nor to new life a dead heart wake.

# UHLAND.

207

# Poems.

## GEDICHTE.

---

## The Minstrel's Curse.

*DES SÄNGER'S FLUCH.*

THERE stood in by-gone ages a castle fair and
 grand,
 It gleamed upon the ocean far out across the land,
Around it fragrant gardens in flowery wreaths
 array'd,
 Wherein the merry fountains in rainbow colors
 play'd.

There sat a haughty monarch who lands and con-
 quests own'd,
 So gloomy and so pallid, that monarch sat en-
 thron'd,

For in his thought lies horror, and scourges in his
  breath,
  And from his eye darts fury, and from his pen
  flows death.

Once came two noble minstrels into this castle fair,
  The locks of one were golden, gray was the
  other's hair ;
A handsome steed the elder did, harp in hand,
  bestride,
  His blooming young companion walked briskly at
  his side.

Then to the youth the elder : " Now be prepared,
  my son,
  Think of our songs most mighty, and choose the
  mightiest one,
Put forth thy rarest powers, both pain and bliss in-
  tone,
  That we to-day may soften the monarch's heart
  of stone."

Now through the columned chamber the minstrels
  both draw nigh,
  The monarch and his lady are there enthroned on
  high ;

The King, like lurid northlight, in awful splendor
gleam'd,
The Queen looked sweet and gentle, as though
the full moon beam'd.

The old bard swept his lyre, swept it with touch so
rare,
That richer, ever richer, the sound rose on the air ;
Anon with heav'nly clearness the youth's voice
flowed along,
And like a ghostly chorus, the old bard's hollow
song.

They sing of love and spring-time, and blissful
golden hours,
Of truth, and faith, and freedom, and manhood's
noblest powers ;
They sing of all the rapture that e'er man's bosom
blest,
Of all the noble yearnings that thrill in human
breast.

Out of the courtiers' glances all scorn has vanished
now,
The King's intrepid warriors to God in homage
bow,

The Queen whose heart has melted, in bliss and
    sadness lost,
    Now down unto the minstrels, the rose from her
        breast has toss'd.

" You have seduced my people, would you now lure
    my queen ? "
    The King all trembling cries it, and glares with
        fearful mien !
He hurls his sword, that, flashing, in the poor youth's
    breast is sheath'd,
    And warm blood gushes forth now, whence golden
        songs were breath'd.

As scattered by a whirlwind the crowd has vanished
    fast,
    Clasped to his master's bosom, the youth has
        breathed his last ;
The master then his mantle about the dead youth
    throws,
    On the steed he binds him upright, and with him
        forth he goes.

But sudden halts the minstrel before the portals tall,
    And then he grasps his lyre,—the rarest of them
        all—

Against a marble pillar he dashes it in twain,
  And shrieks thro' house and gardens this shudder-
    ing refrain :

"Woe is ye, lofty chambers ! Within you never-
    more,
  There shall resound the lyre, or sweet songs as of
    yore,
But only sighs and mourning, and steps of slaves in
    dread,
  Till you lie crushed and mould'ring 'neath the
    avenger's tread.

" Woe is ye, fragrant gardens, all bathed in May's
    soft light,
  This dead, distorted visage I hold up to your
    sight,
That 'neath it you may wither, and all your springs
    run dry,
  O'er-spread with stones, deserted, you may for-
    ever lie.

" Woe is thee ! impious murd'rer ! Thou curse of
    minstrelsy,
  For wreaths of bloody glory thy pains shall fruit-
    less be !

Thy name shall be forgotten, sunk in eternal night,
  And like a last death-rattle, in empty air take
    flight ! "


.        .        .        .        .        .


The gray old bard has cried it, the heavens hear his
    cry,—
  The chambers are demolished, the walls in ruin
    lie,
One lofty column only, past splendor doth recall,
  But that is cleft and, mayhap, o'er night it; too,
    will fall.


.        .        .        .        .        .


Where . once stood fragrant gardens, now lies a
    desert land,
  No tree its shade is spreading, no springs ooze
    thro' the sand,
And of the King's name speaketh nor hero's book,
    nor verse,—
  Sunk under and forgotten ! That is the minstrel's
    curse !

# King Karl on the Sea.

*KÖNIG KARL'S MEERFAHRT.*

KING KARL went sailing o'er the sea
　　By his twelve knights attended :
Out to the Holy Land steered he,
　　When swift a storm descended.

Then spoke that hero bold, Roland :
　　"I fight and fence well, truly,
But all my skill will never stand
　　'Gainst winds and waves unruly."

Sir Holger then—from Denmark he—:
　　" I 've learnt to strike the lyre,
But to what use, when thus the sea
　　And storm are swelling higher?"

Sir Oliver to his weapon turn'd,
　　He too, did not look cheery :
" I 'm much less for myself concern'd
　　Than for the Alteclere."

Then says the wicked Ganelon,—
  His voice he slyly smothers :
" Could only I unharmed get on,
  The devil might take you others."

Archbishop Turpin heaved a sigh :
  " God's cause are we defending ;
Dear Saviour, o'er the sea draw nigh,
  Our voyage safely ending."

Count Richard Fearless, then, quoth he :
  " Ye shades from hellish quarters,
I 've served you often, now help me
  Away from these dread waters."

Sir Naime argued in this wise :
  " I 've counselled many and many ;
Fresh water though, and good advice
  On ships, there 's scarcely any.

The gray Sir Riol : " Old am I,
  And long to battle wedded,
Therefore in dry ground, when I die,
  I 'd have my corpse imbedded."

Sir Guy, a dainty knight was he,
  And he sang forth most sweetly :
" If I a little bird could be,
  I 'd soar to sweetheart fleetly."


" Oh, Lord," cried noble Count Garein,
  " Help us thro' this commotion !
I had much rather drink red wine
  Than water in the ocean."


Sir Lambert then, a lusty youth :
  " Lord, bear in mind our wishes !
I 'd rather eat a fish, forsooth,
  Than be devour'd by fishes."


Sir Gottfried, like a virtuous man,
  Said : " Let what will betide me,
I 'm not more badly treated than
  My brothers all, beside me."


King Karl sits at the rudder, and
  Not one word has he spoken ;
He steers the ship with steady hand
  Till the tempest's force is broken.

# Young Roland.

### KLEIN ROLAND.

DAME BERTHA sat in the cave, and there
    Bewailed her bitter fate;
Young Roland played in the open air,
    His wailing was not great.

" King Karl, oh, noble brother mine,
    Oh, why fled I from thee?
For love did I all state resign,
    Now art thou wroth with me.

" Oh ! Milon, sweetest consort thou,
    Lost in the sea's wild trough !
I cast off all for love,—and now
    By love I am cast off.

" Young Roland, dearest child, in thee
    Rest love and honor now ;
Young Roland, hasten here to me,
    My comfort all art thou.

" Young Roland, now go forth to town,
  To beg for drink and bread ;
For smallest alms, God's thanks call down
  Upon the giver's head."


King Karl sat at the board decked out
  In golden banquet-hall ;
With dish and goblet ran about
  The busy servants all.


Flute, harp, and song with sweetest sound
  All listening hearts then wooed ;
But these clear tones no echoes found
  In Bertha's solitude.


Out in the court a goodly throng
  Of hungry beggars stood ;
Who were less pleased with harp and song
  Than with their drink and food.


Athwart the open door, the King
  Looked down on this array ;
When sudden, thro' the crowded ring
  A fair lad forced his way.

The lad's attire is strange to see,
   Pieced of four shades withal,
But with the beggars lags not he,
   He looks up at the hall.

As tho' he were the castle's lord
   Thro' the hall young Roland stalks,
He lifts a dish up from the board
   And silent out he walks.

The monarch thinks : What do I see ?
   To me this custom 's new.
But as he calmly lets it be,
   The rest permit it too.

A very little while went by, —
   Young Roland again comes up ;
In haste he to the King draws nigh
   And grasps his golden cup.

" Halloo ! hold there, thou saucy wight !"
   The King's words loudly ring ;
Young Roland holds the goblet tight
   And gazes at the King.

The King looked fierce at first, but lo !
   Ere long to smile ẁas seen :
" Thro' this gold hall thou walk'st as tho'
   It were the forest green.

"As one plucks apples from the tree,
   Thou tak'st these dishes mine,
Like water from the fountain free,
   The foam of my red wine."

" The peasants to the fountain come,
   From the tree pluck apples too ;
But game and fish and red wine's foam,
   These are my mother's due."

" If such grand dame thy mother be
   As thou, child, dost maintain,
A lovely castle must have she,
   Also a stately train.

" Tell me who her lord steward is,
   And who that bears her cup ? "
" My right hand her lord steward is,
   My left hand bears her cup."

" Tell me who her true warders be ? "
  " My blue eyes, verily."
" Tell me who is her minstrel free ? "
  " My crimson mouth is he."


" The dame, forsooth, brave servants owns,
  But she likes liveries queer,
Whereon the multi-colored tones
  Like rainbows do appear."


" Eight strong boys have I overcome
  In each ward of the town ;
Four kinds of cloth they brought me home
  As ransom for my gown."


" More faithful than that dame's, I ween,
  Could servant never be ;
No doubt she is a beggar-queen,
  And open house keeps she ?


" For such high dame it were not fair
  Far from my court to bide ;
Well then, three ladies ! Three knights there,
  Up ! Lead her to my side ! "

The cup in haste doth young Roland
　Out from the grand hall take ;
Three maids rise at the King's command,
　Three knights go in their wake.


A very little while went by,—
　The King, far out looks he—
When sudden, in great haste, draw nigh
　The lords and ladies three.


" Help, Heaven ! Can I trust mine eyes ?"
　The King cries suddenly,
" Of my own kin in scoffing wise
　I 've spoken publicly !


" Help Heaven ! Sister Bertha mine,
　In pilgrim's garments gray,
With beggar's staff thro' this hall fine
　Thou drag'st thy weary way !"


Down at his feet then sank the dame,—
　Alas ! pale woman she—
The old rage sudden o'er him came,
　He glared most furiously.

Dame Bertha's glance now quickly falls,
  No word she dares to say ;
Young Roland lifts his gaze, and calls
  His uncle in accents gay.


The King in mild tones thereupon :
  " Arise, O sister, see,
Because of this one, thy dear son,
  Thou shalt forgiven be."


Dame Bertha rose in joyful mood :
  " Dear brother mine, anon
Young Roland shall requite the good
  That thou to me hast done.


" Like to his monarch he shall grow
  To be a hero grand,
Upon his banner and shield shall glow
  The colors of many a land.


" Spoils from the board of many a king
  Shall he seize with his free hand,
Anew to fame and blessings bring
  His sighing fatherland."

# FREILIGRATH.

# Freiligrath.

## Oh! Love as Long as Thou Canst Love!

*O LIEB SO LANG DU LIEBEN KANNST.*

OH ! love as long as thou canst love !
   Oh ! love as long as love will last !
The hour will come, the hour will come,
   When, over graves, thou 'lt mourn the past.

And take good care to keep thy heart
   Aglow with love unceasingly,
As long as in another breast
   A tender love responds to thee.

To him who maketh thee his friend
   Oh ! show all kindness in thy power !
And let no shadow cloud his brow,
   But try to cheer his every hour.

And keep a watch upon thy tongue.
How soon an unkind word is said ;
Oh, God ! it was not meant so ill !—
But now, thy friend, in tears, has fled.


Oh ! love as long as thou canst love !
Oh ! love as long as love will last !
The hour will come, the hour will come,
When, over graves, thou 'lt mourn the past.


Then wilt thou kneel upon the tomb,
And in the high grass, damp and cold,
Thou 'lt hide thine eyes, all dim with tears,—
Thy friend they 'll nevermore behold.


Then wilt thou say : Oh, look on me !
Here at thy grave, I 'm weeping still !
Forgive me if I grieved thee once,—
O God ! it was not meant so ill.


But he can neither see nor hear,
Nor rise to greet thee tenderly ;
The lips that kiss'd thee, ne'er can say
Oh ! long ago I pardoned thee.

Indeed, he pardoned thee long since.
　But burning tears were shed before
For thee and for thy cruel word,—
　But hush,—he sleeps, his journey 's o'er.


Oh ! love as long as thou canst love !
　Oh ! love as long as love will last !
The hour will come, the hour will come,
　When, over graves, thou 'lt mourn the past.

# Rest in the Beloved.

## *RUHE IN DER GELIEBTEN.*

OH ! here forever let me stay, love !
   Here let my resting-place e'er be ;
And both thy tender palms then lay, love,
   Upon my hot brow soothingly.
Here, at thy feet, before thee kneeling,
   In heav'nly rapture let me rest,
And close mine eyes, bliss o'er me stealing,
   Within thine arms, upon thy breast.


I 'll open them but to the glances
   That from thine own in radiance fall ;
The look that my whole soul entrances,
   Oh ! thou who art my life, my all.
I 'll open them but at the flowing
   Of burning tears that upward swell,
And joyously, without my knowing,
   From under drooping lashes well.

Thus am I meek and kind and lowly,
  And good and gentle evermore ;
I have thee—now I 'm blessèd wholly,
  I have thee—now my yearning's o'er.
By thy sweet love intoxicated,
  Within thine arms I 'm lull'd to rest,
And every breath of thine is freighted
  With slumber-songs that soothe my breast.


A life renewed each seems bestowing—
  Oh ! thus to lie day after day,
And hearken with a blissful glowing
  To what each other's heart-beats say.
Lost in our love, entranced, enraptured,
  We disappear from time and space ;
We rest and dream, our souls lie captured
  Within oblivion's sweet embrace.

# In the Woods.

*IM WALDE.*

THROUGH the woods, when dim they 're
grown
My lone path I wend ;
No voice sounds—the trees alone
Softest whispers send.

Oh ! how wide then grows my breast,
And my mind how bright !
Tales I loved in childhood best
Rise before my sight.

Yes, this is a magic haunt !
All that it doth breed,—
Stone and flowers, beast and plant,—
Is bewitched indeed.

In the sun, on leaves of gold,
Coiled, as in a ring,
Musing there, a snake is roll'd,
Daughter of a King.

In the dark pool over there,
  Where the doe has drunk,
Lies her palace, high and fair,
  'Neath the water sunk.

And the king, his consort dear,
  All their retinue,
Also many a cavalier,
  Those depths hide from view.

And the hawk, who 's e'er at hand,
  Poising o'er the dell,
Is the sorcerer, whose wand
  Weaves this magic spell.

Were the word revealed to me
  To undo this charm,
She at once redeemed should be
  Clasp'd within my arm.

From the serpent's skin she 'd rise
  Crownèd radiantly,
Thanks on lips, and in her eyes,
  Sweet timidity.

From the pool then would emerge
   Straight, the castle old ;
While upon its banks would surge
   Troops of warriors bold.


With her king, the ancient queen
   Then would greet our sight ;
'Neath a velvet baldachin
Would they sit, while tree-tops green
   Trembled with delight.


And the hawk, whom gently now
   Clouds and breeze caress,
In the dust should be laid low,
   Crush'd and powerless.


Sylvan-gladness, sylvan-rest !
   Fairy-visions bright !
Oh ! how you refresh my breast,
   And my rhymes invite !

# RÜCKERT.

235

# Rückert.

---

## I Love Thee, for 't is Thee, Dear, I Must Love !

*ICH LIEBE DICH WEIL ICH DICH LIEBEN MUSS.*

I LOVE thee, for 't is thee, dear, I must love,
   I love thee, dear, for I must needs love thee,
I love thee by decree of heav'n above,
   I love thee 'neath the spell of sorcery !

'T is thee I love, as loves its bush the rose,
   As loves the sun the light which he doth give,
'T is thee I love, for thy breath in me glows,
   'T is thee I love, for in that love I live !

# The Nightingale.

*DIE NACHTIGALL.*

AS nightingale, at nightfall
  A home on earth I found ;
My young heart soon acquired,
  By sorrow's strength inspired,
Its song's melodious sound.


But gloomy was the thicket
  Wherein I dwelt alone ;
No master there to teach me,
  No hearer's praise could reach me,  ·
My songs remained unknown.


'T is true, I dreamed that yonder,
  A brilliant world must be ;
I longed but once to see it,
  And then fore'er to flee it,—
That was not granted me.

But then there came a spirit
　To show me life, at last,
And now,—by life surrounded,
　I 'd leave it, for I 've found it
A cage that holds me fast.


Why do we never value
　Our blessings till they 're o'er ?
Who will, through life's delusion,
　Lead me, to the seclusion
Of my dear woods, once more ?

# MÖRICKE.

# Moericke.

## An hour Ere Break of Day.

*EIN STÜNDLEIN WOHL VOR TAG.*

AS I once sleeping lay,
   An hour ere break of day,
Sang near the window, on a tree,
   A little bird—scarce heard by me—
An hour ere break of day.

" Give heed to what I say :
   Thy sweetheart false doth play,
Whilst I am singing this to thee,
   He hugs a maiden, cosily,
An hour ere break of day."

"Alas ! no further say !
   Hush ! I 'll not hear thy lay !
Fly off, away fly from my tree,—
   Ah ! love and faith are mockery,
An hour ere break of day."

# CHAMISSO.

245

# Chamisso.

## Woman's Love and Life.

*FRAUENLIEBE UND LEBEN.*

### I.

SINCE mine eyes beheld him
   Blind, methinks, I 've grown,
Wheresoe'er I turn them,
   Him I see alone !

O'er me floats his image
   As in waking dreams,
Thro' the deepest darkness
   Brighter still it gleams.

All else that surrounds me
  Gloomy is, and bare ;
For my sisters' pastimes
  I no longer care.

Rather in my chamber
  Would I weep alone—
Since mine eyes beheld him
  Blind, methinks, I 've grown !

## II.

He, the lordliest of all mortals,
  He so gentle, he so kind !
Sweetest lips and brightest glances,
  Valor firm, and lucid mind !

As from azure depths there glitters
  Bright and glorious yonder star,
Thus shines he down from my heaven,
  Bright and glorious, high and far.

Wander, wander, in thy orbit,
  Let me but thy radiance see,
Let me meekly but behold it,—
  Blessèd then, and sad I 'll be.

Take no heed of my still prayer,
  Offered for thy happiness,
Durst not know thy humble servant,
  Thou high star of lordliness !

For thy choice must honor only
  Her, who 's worthiest of all,
On that lofty maid my blessings
  Many thousand times should fall.      .

Then I 'll weep, but I 'll be happy !
  Blessèd, blessèd then my lot.
And although my heart be breaking,—
  Break, oh, heart ! it matters not !

### III.

I cannot grasp or believe it, ·
  My soul by a dream has been sway'd !
How could he have, over all others,
  Exalted and bless'd me, poor maid ?

It seemed as though he had spoken :
  " I am thine through eternity ! "
It seemed—oh ! still I am dreaming,
  For thus it never can be.

Oh ! let me thus dreaming expire,
   As on his bosom I sink !
In tears of unspeakable rapture
   The happiest death there to think.

www.ingramcontent.com/pod-product-compliance
Lightning Source LLC
Chambersburg PA
CBHW020348030726
47496CB00007B/2059